A+W

As Empty
As Hate

By the same author:

THREE FOR ADVENTURE
FOUR FIND DANGER
TWO MEET TROUBLE
HEIR TO MURDER
MURDER COMES HOME
WHO SAW HIM DIE?
MURDER BY THE WAY
FOUL PLAY SUSPECTED
WHO DIED AT THE GRANGE?
FIVE TO KILL
MURDER AT KING'S KITCHEN
WHO SAID MURDER?
CRIME WITH MANY VOICES
NO CRIME MORE CRUEL
MURDER MAKES MURDER
MYSTERY MOTIVE
FIRST A MURDER
LEND A HAND TO MURDER
NO END TO DANGER
WHO KILLED REBECCA?
THE DYING WITNESSES
MURDER WEEK-END
DINE WITH MURDER
QUARREL WITH MURDER

The Jane Brothers books:
TAKE A BODY
LAME DOG MURDER
MURDER IN THE STARS
MAN ON THE RUN

OUT OF THE SHADOWS
DEATH OUT OF DARKNESS
CAT AND MOUSE
MURDER AT END HOUSE
RUNAWAY
DEATH OF A STRANGER
MURDER ASSURED
MISSING FROM HOME
THICKER THAN WATER
HOW MANY TO KILL?
GO AHEAD WITH MURDER
THE MAN I KILLED
THE EDGE OF TERROR
HATE TO KILL
GUILT OF INNOCENCE

The Dr. Cellini books:
CUNNING AS A FOX
WICKED AS THE DEVIL
SLY AS THE SERPENT
CRUEL AS A CAT
TOO GOOD TO BE TRUE
A PERIOD OF EVIL
AS LONELY AS THE DAMNED

A Falcon's Head Mystery

As Empty As Hate

John Creasey
as Kyle Hunt

WORLD PUBLISHING
TIMES MIRROR
NEW YORK

Published by The World Publishing Company
Published simultaneously in Canada
by Nelson, Foster & Scott Ltd.
First American edition

First printing—1972

Copyright © 1972 by John Creasey
All rights reserved
ISBN 0-529-04486-2
Library of Congress catalog card number: 77-185118
Printed in the United States of America

WORLD PUBLISHING
TIMES MIRROR

CONTENTS

Chapter		Page
1	Woman in Fear	7
2	Strangers	16
3	Vanessa	28
4	The Growing Hate	37
5	Discussion	46
6	Near Death	56
7	To Let Her Die?	65
8	Morning	75
9	Questions	85
10	First Visit	94
11	Dr. Emmanuel Cellini	104
12	Three Plus One	112
13	Fury	123
14	Uneasy Peace	133
15	The Turret Room	143
16	Threat of Burning	153
17	The Sightseers	162
18	Lie?	172
19	A Matter of Trespass	181

Chapter One

WOMAN IN FEAR

She watched them from the window.

She had feared the truth for a long while; and now she knew it beyond all question: knew that she had lost her husband; lost the man she had loved for almost as long as she could remember; and she knew, deep within her, that she had lost him for all time.

She thought: I hate her.

They came, Vanessa and Jacob, walking towards the house. Vanessa was laughing, Vanessa was happy, as happy as she was beautiful, her hair so fair, her face so gay. Oh God, dear God, don't let me hate her.

She thought: *I do hate her.*

There she was with her hair tossed back, her eyes so bright and blue they seemed like sunlit sea. Oh God, dear God, don't let me hate her.

She thought: *I could kill her.*

She stood so tall, above Jacob's shoulder, as she looked up into his eyes, reading, pleading. What did she read in his long, strong face? What was the pleading in the stillness of those moments? Was she pleading, please don't go in, don't go back to her, stay here and come with me, never let me go again, my darling, oh my darling. And what was Jacob saying with his eyes hidden from the watcher? Was he saying that he must go back to his wife and duty, to the mother of his children, to the place that had been home?

Was he showing his yearning for this new and so bright love? Was he trying to tell Vanessa all she needed was to be patient? That all she had to do was wait a while, days or weeks or even months, until the time came when he would come with her?

Suddenly their hands moved, Jacob's and Vanessa's; standing up here by the curtained window, Anne could see the way they gripped, sense their tension. See her loved one loose his grip, see the pain in Vanessa's eyes as the lovers parted, see the torment in her husband's face as he turned and left Vanessa. See her stand and stare at his broad back, then turn and walk so fast that she was almost running.

Then such pain as she herself had never known caught at heart and throat and lungs, sending a dark blindness across her eyes so that she saw neither of them any more. Oh God, dear dear God, please don't let me hate her.

I hate her.

*　　*　　*

Jacob entered his house, and closed the door, very quietly.

It was a house of medium size, standing in its own two acres, rare amid the bungalows and the red-brick houses spread about King's Narrows. Beyond and at both sides were trees, centuries-old oak and beech growing on land precious to him because it had been his family's for many generations, precious to the builders who had spawned their chalet designs and their ranch-type houses up almost to the branches. On his land they could build another dozen, and for his land they had offered him a fortune.

He was not thinking of that now.

He was thinking of Vanessa, and of Anne.

Also, he was thinking of his yearning as much as of his

folly; and of the ache consuming him by night and day.

He went into the drawing-room and stepped close to the window, hoping to catch a last glimpse of Vanessa. It had been folly to arrange to meet her so near here, close enough to disturb the almost-peace of the house and grounds; but her coming, like their love, had a kind of inevitability, and now for the first time he wondered just where it would take them.

He saw Vanessa, and his heart leapt. She was walking beyond a group of trees that fringed the field where a group of hippies were camping. He watched her pass the gap in the hawthorn hedge between his land and the houses of the new estate. She looked back. She was too far away to see him clearly, but no doubt could see the house with its weathered brick and tall windows.

Then she turned and walked on, and his heart fell as she passed from sight.

These were simple, physical facts. The sight of her, although at a distance and although she was going away and they might conceivably never see each other again, had made his heart seem light; but the moment she disappeared he felt as if he had a cold stone inside him.

There had been a time when he had thought talk of such human reactions to be absurd, dubbing them fantasies woven in starved minds craving for romance. Or else, he had thought they were only for the very young. At such moments he had wondered if he had ever been young. Now, he knew that the emotions were real and vivid and all-absorbing for him, and for Vanessa. They were realities. Being in love with Vanessa Belhampton was as real as being married to Anne, as living here, as having comfort and a little pride of possession and even some sense of affection. These real things, now, were close together, comforting him, and he sensed that one day, soon, he would have to choose between them.

He tried to shut the mood out of his mind, but it would not go.

He turned from the window, but as he reached the door, he tensed. He might find Anne just outside, or approaching. He would have to explain why he had been in the room; or else, wonder whether she suspected what had happened to him.

That fear was born of his guilt.

If he had gone into the room, as he had so often done years ago, to look at a bird or squirrel more closely, he wouldn't have thought twice about telling her. But he had gone simply to see Vanessa, and he could not tell Anne so. There were so many things he could not tell her these days. Harsh, hurtful things drawn out of his own hurts and unhappiness. Yet, when thinking of them, even when talking to Vanessa about them, he would have flashes of doubt. Was he seeing a newly experienced truth, or had it been the truth in the early and succeeding days of his marriage?

How much of his past unhappiness was true? And how much of it was a reflection of this new, devastating happiness he had found with Vanessa?

He did not know.

He could not remember the time when he had not known Anne. She had been born in a house long since demolished by builders' greed and people's need of homes. He had seen her a few days after she had been born, wizened — as he had since learned all babies were — with thin black hair. A *Navajo!* he had cried in his simplicity, for he had been seven years old and freshly back from his visits to his grandparents in America's New Mexico and Arizona and the great and beautiful waste lands of the Navajo reserves.

Baby Anne, who had fascinated him.

Child Anne; of whom he had been fond.

Teenage Anne; with her glorious eyes and early signs of maturity.

Seductive Anne.

But had she been seductive? Or had it been simply her beauty which had seduced him? For she had been nineteen and he twenty-six, old enough to know the implications and the responsibilities of taking this daughter of a neighbour and close friend to bed. Seducing her? Betraying her? Whatever the phrase used, in the mind or on the lip, there was ugliness. It carried a sense of failed responsibility — and so of guilt. From the moment she had lain beneath him that first time, so eager and yet so frightened, so still and suddenly so passionate, creating a maelstrom of which he was only part of the power, he had committed himself to marrying her.

That had been why he had lived so long in a mood of revulsion. He had known exaltation when he had been with her, but the thought of marriage had brought a chill fear, made no less because the obligation had been his fault.

His? Or hers?

How could he honestly say, twenty-five years after, that it had been hers? That she had seduced him knowing the inevitability of marriage to follow, not that he had seduced her, driven to desire because of the milk-white softness of her body.

He — *they* — had been drawn into a kind of vortex; showered with the blessing of both mothers and both fathers, told by hint and innuendo that marriage between the families was everyone's heart's desire; at last, promise, plans, wedding, marriage, and all the time, as he remembered —

As he remembered?

Did he truly remember or had he superimposed a kind of fantasy of what he wanted to be true in retrospect? Had he really approached the marriage with grave misgivings? Had he really wanted to break the engagement and been prevented by the emotional pressures of the inevitable disapproval of the parents, and the hurt that Anne would suffer? Had the forces crowding on him really forced him to the marriage? And had he truly hated it almost from the very first day?

Were these things true?

Was he being honest with himself when he thought them true? Was he being fair to Anne? If they were true, how could he stay with her? If they were lies, made to excuse the way he felt for Vanessa, then how could he leave her and live with his black conscience?

These thoughts stayed with him like close and hated companions. Day in and day out he wrestled with them; and each day they seemed more painful because each day brought him closer to decision: should he, and could he bring himself to, leave his wife?

The question and the arguments were with him as he walked and worked and talked, as he laughed and as he smiled; they were like shadows ever-present, and the sun which caused them was Vanessa.

He went out of the drawing-room, to an empty hall. Thank God: an empty staircase and passage, an empty breakfast room. Beyond, in the kitchen, Dulcie was working, he could hear the movement of pots and pans; Dulcie, nearly seventy, had always been noisy in the kitchen. He walked along the passage between the kitchen and the scullery and washroom, and opened the heavy door. There was Dulcie, her short grey hair on end, capable, sturdy, wielding a rolling pin with great precision.

"Hallo, Dulcie!"

"Why, Mr. Jacob, you scared me."

"Is Mrs. Anne about?"

"I think she's in the house, sir."

"Then I'll go and look for her," Jacob said. "What's for dinner tonight?"

"Saddle of lamb, sir, and new potatoes and peas from the garden."

"And mint sauce, mind you."

"Go on with you," she said. "Have I ever forgotten the mint sauce?"

He laughed on her indignation, thinking: Vanessa loves mint sauce. Vanessa. He went back to the front of the house, hesitating, then opened the door of his study which was opposite the foot of the stairs, and went inside. He wanted to be alone. He had to see Anne but he wanted to be alone, as he always did unless he were with Vanessa. There was solitude in the study. It was a resting place and sanctuary, where he could sit and read and think and dream, and even — these days — work. His thoughts went off at a tangent although the main theme was the same: the searching within himself for the truth. He had accepted his life without question for so long that now he had begun to question it, he never stopped.

Was his marriage really at the root of his trouble? Or was the fact that he did not need to work, that whenever he did work it was because he was driven by his conscience — man *should* work — the main cause?

Oh, to hell with conscience!

What was he? Son of puritans, son of the godly?

He went inside the study but did not close the door. It was a pleasant room. Two walls were lined with books from floor to ceiling, and while some were leather-bound most were in their bright and colourful jackets. A third wall was nearly all window, with curtains at either side, seldom drawn. His desk was in front of the fourth wall, on which were photographs of his family and pictures he loved and a few trophies he had won — years ago — for swimming. He so seldom swam now, and only occasionally bathed in the pool that shimmered at the top of the garden. The house was on the brow of King's Narrows and on either side the land fell away. Here roses grew in profusion, and beyond, fruit trees. The pool lay beside a silver birch and one great oak.

He sat on the arm of his reading chair, looking out of the window, unseeing.

He was so very much alone.

He did not know when he would next see Vanessa; certainly not until he had seen Anne. His hands were gripping tightly, nails biting into the palms; his teeth were clenching painfully and his whole body was on edge, at the thought of facing his wife.

He heard footsteps overhead.

This room was immediately beneath the nursery, now occupied only occasionally by one of their three children when there was a big family or house-party and the house was full to overflowing. It had the same outlook as the study, but being that much higher the view extended beyond the pool to the new houses, built where Anne's old house had been. Standing up at that window, she would be looking back over her past; their past.

What went on in her mind?

Had she ever been really happy, married to him?

He felt a momentary lightening of heart at the flash of hope; hope that she, too, was tired of the marriage; that she, too, had been hiding the truth of unhappiness from him; that the news that he wanted a divorce so that he could marry Vanessa might bring relief to her. It was even possible that she had a lover.

He toyed with this hope for a few moments, but it soon died. He knew better. She had known no man but him. She still loved, wanted, and possessed him. She would never divorce him willingly, and would fight against him divorcing her.

But he couldn't be sure.

With that thought, he reflected: she might be glad for me to go. There's only one way to find out. Sooner or later I have to ask her.

Why not tonight?

*   *   *

Anne thought: he knows I'm up here, but he doesn't call me and doesn't come up. He doesn't want to see me, he simply wants to be with her.

She stood looking over the past which seemed to be reflected in the pool, and the prayer which had clutched at her when she had stood and watched them seemed to roar through her mind: oh God, dear God, don't let me hate her.

But she did hate Vanessa.

Suddenly, she put into spoken words what was now so vividly in her mind. "I could kill her." The words actually made sound. She added to them: "If she takes him away from me, I could kill her."

And then: "If she takes him away from me, I *will* kill her!"

Into the silence which followed the whisper there came the sound of Jacob's footsteps on the stairs.

Chapter Two

STRANGERS

Jacob saw Anne's shadow as she moved. She appeared with the light behind her, making a halo about her hair. She was beautiful, yet with a cold beauty, remote, as that of a stranger. When he spoke her name, it was with an effort.

"Anne," he said. "I wondered where you were."

* * *

The light from window and doorway fell on his hatchet-sharp face and on his greying hair; on his lean handsomeness. It fell on his steel-grey eyes which should have lit up, had he been approaching a woman he loved. Her gaze ran over every line of his face, that she knew so well. In a way it was like looking at these dear, familiar things as from a distance. Over them was a kind of glaze, as if life had fled from them.

It was like looking at someone long-remembered.

It was like hearing a voice from which all the life and vibrancy had been drawn.

"Anne, I wondered where you were."

"I've been up here," she said, as flatly.

"Yes, I see."

"I've been remembering," she told him.

"It must be full of memories for you."

"For *me*?" she asked, with bitterness he could not fail to hear.

"For us, but mostly for you," he replied.

"I suppose so."

"It's funny," he began, only to stop abruptly.

"What's funny?" she asked, as if nothing in the world could ever be funny again.

He moistened his lips.

"To think all three children have gone," he said.

"Funny?" she echoed. "Is that all you find it?"

"Do you miss them so much?"

"Of course I do," Anne said. "They were all I had." And after a pause she went on, with tears in her voice: "Oh, Tony, darling Tony." She paused again and then looked accusingly at Jacob, and said in a hard voice: "You drove him away. You drove him away because you knew I loved him, and you hated the thought of my being happy."

He thought: She drove him away and she always blames me.

And he thought: What is the use of arguing over and over again?

* * *

Three children, two girls and a boy. Angela and Joan and Anthony, twenty-three, twenty-one, nineteen. Angela the gayest, the liveliest, the noisiest, the one they had needed to worry about least, now in Australia with a husband and twins. Angela, for joy! Joan, the pale and gentle one, who made them anxious for her well-being in a pushing, advertising world. Joan, too, married and away, carried off by the tall, bronzed, second cousin from the New Mexican desert, to the land of the Navajos. Joan, brought to life by love and being loved, bursting into beauty.

And Anthony.

Anthony...

"I know you'll both hate it," he had said, "but I'm going to teach in Africa."

"But *why*?" Anne had cried, unable to hide her anguish.

"I don't know," he had lied. "I feel I can do some good there. I can't do any here. I — I don't feel right in England."

That was when Jacob had made his great mistake.

He and Anthony had never really got on, never really understood each other. But what father and son ever have understood each other? What parents, and what children? The awful thing was that in a way Tony had been used by Anne as a weapon against him; in another way, used by him as a weapon against her.

It was awful to remember back so many years; to the first stirrings of hatred. And although hatred was at times too strong a word there were moments when there seemed to be no other to describe what they had come to feel for each other.

Hate; love; hate.

He had so wanted a boy; she had wanted girls. So the first two children had pleased her, and he had come to love them both so that it had ceased to matter.

But she could not leave it alone. She probed. Not deep thrusts; not really barbs; but little darts which, when he was in the mood, would sting. And she had seemed even then to choose moments when, for one reason or another, he was over-sensitive. Just after they had had a quarrel, perhaps; or when the McNamaras had had one of their interminable sons.

And then, on every kind of excuse, she would deny him her body.

"Oh, Jacob. I'm so tired...You know I can't tonight... It's no use, I've a terrible headache." And then, such a fuss and trouble over contraceptives. Had the Pill been available in those days, she would have fought against it with all her will. *"Nothing's safe, and you know I don't want another baby."*

To this day, he marvelled that Anthony had been conceived; but there had been odd hours, sometimes odd days, when they had touched happiness. Afterwards, almost daily, she had been tearful and fearful. *"I can't stand another baby, I can't, I tell you... You've got to do something... Sean won't, you know he won't, he's a Catholic!"* He, Jacob, had even gone to their doctor and friend, Sean McNamara.

"I'm sorry, Jacob. It's not a matter of religious principle. It's purely medical. Anne is perfectly capable of having a baby, and it will probably do her much more good than harm."

They were the months when Anne had first uttered a threat to kill herself. But she had not made the slightest attempt.

"Don't worry, Jacob. When she's got the baby, everything will be all right," Sean had soothed.

And for a while, for a few months, it was so, for the child was Anthony, and he doted on it, and Anne appeared happy enough with the child. "Absolutely no more," she would say, "but he's lovely."

And then she began to get jealous. She would stop Jacob from taking the boy from his pram; accuse him of hurting him; accuse him of feeding him too quickly or too slowly. Of being too rough; of pulling bedclothes up too close to his chin. And later, of letting him out of doors when it was too cold, of driving too fast, of fussing him too much, of not giving him enough attention. The only time of real relief had been when Tony was away at school; at least, she conceded that he should go first to Loftus Hall, then to

Galeston, his schools. Just what happened at Galeston, Jacob didn't know, would never know.

"I am desperately sorry," the headmaster had said, "but marijuana was found in your son's possession. Three other boys had it in their possession, also. And I've no choice, no choice at all. They must all be expelled."

So, Jacob had brought Tony home, before trying to reason with him.

"But Tony — why did you do it?... Have you smoked much?... Where did you get it?.... Will you promise not to smoke it again?..."

It had been no good, of course, Anthony had simply refused to answer, refused to talk, and then Anne had come to his defence. He wanted help, not understanding. He needed treatment... Sean McNamara would help him.

So, Anthony had been to see Sean. It had been a long session, an agonising day at home while Jacob and Anne had waited. Then, Sean had telephoned, and said very simply:

"He's a rebel, but he's not an addict of the drug, Jacob... What he needs is a job, a hard one preferably, to try to sink himself into. It wouldn't hurt him to get a job away from home."

"No!" Anne had cried. "He's got to be near home, where I can look after him."

Later, there had been fierce arguments and finally a furious quarrel about the boy; all the venom they had stored up came out, and Anne had shown herself at her hysterical worst. They had not realised that Tony had overheard. A few weeks later he had made his decision to leave England and go to Africa.

* * *

Anne blamed him, Jacob.
And he blamed Anne.
But they were both to blame.

Did Anne ever admit that to herself, Jacob wondered. Did she know that together she and Jacob had driven the boy away? Did she know that the atmosphere at King's Narrows had stifled him until he could not breathe? Did she suspect, as he suspected, that the lure of far-off places had taken the girls, too; that they had never been happy here nor seen how they ever could be. Did she know that her possessiveness had crippled them as it had crippled him?

Or was he lying to himself? Making excuses for himself; making her an ogre, an evil creature with whom no one could live? Was he simply justifying himself, and his new love and his desperate desire to get away? The children were all she had had, she just said, but had she possessed them any more than she possessed him? Flesh of her flesh, blood of her blood, but were they of her heart and mind? Slowly he brought himself out of the past which in some ways was more vivid than the present.

"I'm sorry," he said lamely.

"Are you?"

"I mean — I'm sorry I pretended not to know."

"Not to know what?"

"How much you miss the children."

He had come to her convinced that this was the moment to tell her the truth; if it had been, then it was fading, if it had not already gone. He was doing what he had done so often: soothing her, trying to reassure her, being desperately sorry for her and hating to add to hurt.

"As if there could be any doubt," she said.

"We hear from them all," he said.

"Oh, yes. We hear."

"They're very good, as today's young people go," Jacob claimed.

"They're like all young people," she said. "They want to lead a life of their own."

He almost choked: "Well — it's natural. *We* did."

"I don't blame them," Anne said. "I'd set so much store by having them near, but I don't blame them."

"They'll come back from time to time."

They were empty words, like all the words between them. It was so often so but today the emptiness was more apparent. He put it down to his own ultra-sensitivity. He thought she looked beautiful with her dark hair and regular features; a little Italian, perhaps, or Spanish: not the English that knowledge of her forebears might have suggested. Was she ill? He had thought often during their marriage that whenever crisis threatened she had appeared to be. Was it deliberately imposed? There was no heartiness in her although there was a toughness; she could be strong whenever she wanted to be.

Now, he was almost as tongue-tied as with a stranger.

"Shall we go downstairs?" he asked.

"What time is it?"

"About six, I suppose. Would you care for a swim?"

She hesitated. She was looking at him with great intensity, pursing her lips a little, and he was apprehensive, without quite knowing why. Then suddenly her expression changed, and she said quite brightly:

"Yes, that's a good idea. Shall we?"

"Yes!" It was something to do, an excuse for trivia. "I won't be a jiff!" He stood aside for her to pass on the landing, she into her room, he into his dressing-room where he now slept. She gave him a near-coquettish glance as she disappeared.

Soon, in a white Terry-towelling robe, with a green patterned towel over his arm, dark swimming trunks on, he called from her door, which stood ajar:

"Ready, there?"

"Nearly," she called. "Come and wait a moment."

He pushed the door open and went inside, in time — as instantly he felt sure that she intended — to see her at the door of her bathroom.

Naked.

She had the most beautiful body. Peerless. So pale and so unblemished, with every curve somehow seductive, every attitude and every movement studied. Now she was looking over her left shoulder: coquettishly was the only word. Her long hair fell to her shoulders emphasising her nakedness.

She disappeared, and the door closed.

He wanted to leave, even to run. He wanted to get away from here, from her, from all hint or obligation of intimacy. But if he went out of the room, what an insult it would be to her pride, the particular pride she had always felt in her body. She knew its power, as she had always known it. He could remember the day in this house, when they had been left alone, by chance; when he had first seen her.

It had been much then as it was now.

She *had* seduced him!

His heart began to beat very fast, a positive hammering, because on that instant he knew the truth. She, not he, had been the seducer. And, if she had her way, still would be.

When he heard her again he was almost afraid to turn round, but there was no need. She had on a towelling kimono, with huge yellow flowers on a white background, falling halfway down her thighs. She carried a matching towel and a scarlet cap. Her hair was coiled up loosely on top of her head in an attractively careless-seeming way, and she smiled quite naturally.

"Ready?"

"Ready!"

They moved out to the landing.

"It's a perfect afternoon for a bathe."

"Perfect."

She took his hand. He sensed what she was going to do, and so steeled himself not to draw his away. Going down the stairs, they were perforce very close.

"It's a long time since we had a swim together," she remarked.

"The weather's been so bad."

"But today's been lovely."

Empty, empty, empty words, empty of all meaning. What had possessed him ever to think they could have significance? Empty, boring, artificial, words for the sake of words: trivia upon trivia. Sometimes it had nearly driven him crazy. But there *had* been the children, and her beauty, and a kind of superficial brilliance she could sometimes show. And there had been friends and relatives in great variety, for they had always kept open house.

Why did the friends come so seldom these days?

They went past the dining-room and study and along a narrow passage to the side door, which faced west. The sun struck warm. They both wore rubber-soled sandals, making them impervious to gravel-path or stone. The early geraniums in the beds near the house were lovely, and the sweeping lawns were beautifully kept. They walked over grass towards the fruit trees and the pool.

"We're going to have a wonderful crop of apples this year," she remarked.

"Best for ages," he agreed.

"I'll race you," she challenged, and began to run.

As she ran she peeled off the robe, and let it fall behind her on to the grass. She wore some flimsy kind of bikini, marked like a leopard's skin. Without looking round she reached the pool and stood poised, slipping her cap over her hair, tucking in a few strands, and then raised her arms, ready to dive.

What was the matter with him, that her body could so

stir him even now, and her mind and her nature either repel or leave him cold?

As he drew up she dived in. There was hardly a splash. She went under smoothly and came up as smoothly, turning on her back with the grace of a porpoise. In most sports, she was poor, having a lack of co-ordination which had often puzzled him, but she was at home in the water. She floated, beckoning him. She had done this often, in the more distant past, and he sensed that she was reaching back into the past, trying to recapture the mood she had felt and he had pretended to.

He had enjoyed swimming with her at one time, but usually it had been with others, later with the children and their friends. She formed the words: "Come on in" with her lips. He slid out of his robe and, trying to enter into the spirit of the moment, ran to the side and dived in. He did not know that running he also looked magnificent; that although in clothes he sometimes seemed too thin, stripped, his pale body — every muscle of his torso, arms and legs in play — gleamed almost god like. He hit the water as cleanly as Anne had done, swam beneath her, and came up on the other side. He shook the water off his wiry hair and out of his eyes.

She was just in front of him.

"Good?"

"Very good."

"Race you," she said again. "Two lengths."

"Four," he countered.

"All right, four."

The water was a little warmer than the air, and both were pleasant. Anne won by a yard or more, and clung to the edge, laughing. The bikini covered only the under-swell and nipples of her breasts. She was gasping a little for breath, and so was he.

"Another?" she asked.
"I'll do some diving."
"I'll swim," she decided.

For ten or fifteen minutes they disported themselves, and anyone watching would have sworn that they were not only enjoying every moment but were happy. It was Anne who got out first. She draped her towel round her shoulders and then stood watching as he made another dive.

His heart had suddenly gone cold. He knew what she wanted: for him to join her, step behind her, then place his hands on the towel and press it against her body, drying her and at the same time becoming excited by her. Had she planned this from the moment he had suggested swimming? He stayed under water, these thoughts flooding his mind. If he did not respond to her obvious invitation, then it would probably lead to an angry mood, sharp, painful words, a miserable dinner and more miserable evening. If he did what she wanted then inevitably it would lead to a sensuous mood of hoped-for lovemaking. If he made love with his body, repugnance in his mind and hatred in his heart, then an icy mood of recrimination would follow. There would be an ugly scene, perhaps argument going long into the night.

He hauled himself out of the water, still undecided, while she waited for him, the towel slipping enticingly off her shoulders.

* * *

She thought with an almost shrill vehemence: He's mine.

She took the male beauty of his body for granted; it was hers.

There was nothing she would not do for him, she loved him so much that there was pangs of passion in her very breathing. *He was hers.* No one was going to take him away from her.

And this moment was hers, too.

She was sure that he could not resist her; that soon he would move behind her and his arms would encircle her and she would lean back against him, almost purring with the pleasure of his caress. This was going to be her night: *their* night. She would show him what ecstasy they could share, would drive away all thought of that golden-haired bitch from his mind.

He drew near. Something in his expression warned her that he was undecided. She felt a searing stab of hate for the other woman.

She thought: I'll kill her before I'll let her take him away from me.

Then, he stepped behind her. There seemed a long, agonising wait, before his hands fell upon her, and raised the towel and began to press. She could not see the anguish on his face in the moment of defeat. Even as he touched her, he saw Vanessa in his mind's eye.

Vanessa might be home by now, in the heart of London.

Chapter Three

VANESSA

Vanessa turned into Langdon Square, with its tall, porticoed houses, the round pillars at every porch, the white paint and the shiny black, giving the houses a kind of austerity softened by the small, iron-fenced garden in the middle. At one end were two silver birches which reminded her of the trees in Jacob's garden.

Jacob!

She uttered his name; she could picture his face in those times when he was gay and carefree, at the beginning of a meeting, long before the sadness of parting began to touch his sharp features with shadow. He was like a hawk, with eyes as vivid bright. She turned into the porchway of the house where she and Mercia and their mother and father lived, and took out her key. As she pushed the door open, Mercia appeared at the foot of the stairs.

"My!" exclaimed Mercia, "you *do* look happy. Have you come into a fortune?"

Vanessa closed the door, hesitated only for a second, then went towards her sister with her arms outstretched.

"No," she said. "But I'm in love!" She put her arms round Mercia and led her into a few gay steps of a waltz, then gave her a hug and drew back. Both were laughing, and Vanessa felt a sweep of happiness which was born of being with Jacob. "In love, in love, in love!" she repeated with her heart echoing in her voice.

At the top of the stairs her mother was standing, looking down, smiling; the daughters did not realise she was there. The house, with its tall ceilings, spacious rooms and beautiful furniture, was bright and warm. Priceless paintings covered the walls, enhanced by the delicate colouring of the Persian carpets beneath. The sisters stood for a moment silently, Mercia dark and half-a-head shorter, Vanessa like a Diana with her hair swept back from her forehead as if wind were whistling past her.

"Vanessa," Mercia said at last, "I'm so glad!"

"Mercy," said Vanessa, huskily, "it's so wonderful, so good."

"I wondered," Mercy began, and stopped short, for though they were close in some ways, there were others when they were far apart; each had a life the other did not probe. "Oh, I'm so glad," she said again.

"Vanessa," their mother called, and began to come down the stairs.

At sixty she had a figure to rival Mercia's, and a poise which seemed to have been born in her. Vanessa stood at the foot of the stairs, her arms outstretched.

"Vanessa," her mother said. "I am so happy for you Who is he, my darling?"

Vanessa, laughter sparkling, said: "A man."

"Well, how remarkable," exclaimed Lady Belhampton. She turned to Mercia. "Your sister has fallen in love with a man."

"We were always a peculiar family," observed Mercia, solemnly.

"Do we know this man of your affections?" asked Lady Belhampton.

And Vanessa said: "No, mother. No."

A shadow crossed her face and touched both her mother and her sister. She was aware of them both looking at her, steadily, questioningly. And in those moments she realised that she would have to tell them the truth, and she was not sure how they would respond. Could one really know so little about one's family, about those whom one had loved all one's life? The stillness as they stood together seemed touched with profundity, until their mother broke it.

"Do you want to talk about it, Vanessa?"

"I won't stay —" Mercia began.

"Please!" Vanessa exclaimed, and startled them both. She gave a little laugh, and then went on: "I'd like to tell you both." She turned, they with her, into the front room, a beautiful room which could, but did not, have seemed stiff and formal because of the priceless antiques in it. At one side, near the Adam fireplace, stood a wide couch drawn up so that three or four or even five could sit and talk in comfort. Here their mother and Mercia sat, while Vanessa sank into a winged Regency armchair. "I've been wanting to tell you for a long time," she went on. "But I had to be absolutely certain before I did."

Her mother smiled. "Certain of yourself, dear, or certain of him?"

Vanessa half-laughed. "Both," she answered.

"And now you are sure?"

"Yes," said Vanessa. "I'm sure of us both." She laced her fingers, tightening a grip because it was so difficult to go on. "He —"

"Is he married?" asked her mother, and her eyes asked for the truth, but Mercia's closed, momentarily, in a kind of fear.

"Yes," answered Vanessa.

"Happily?" her mother asked.

"No," answered Vanessa, still more huskily. "Not if —"

She broke off, surprised how difficult it was to talk, to say what came to her mind without giving them a wrong impression.

"Not if he's told you the truth," her mother said, in the softest of voices.

"I think he has," Vanessa declared.

"Can't you be sure?" demanded Mercia, almost angrily.

"It's really — can he be sure," Vanessa corrected. "And I think he is."

"Oh, indeed!" exclaimed Mercia. She knew her own weaknesses, which was why she had offered to leave the other two alone. She was, of all the family, the most conventional. And she had been widowed, four years ago, leaving her for a while desolate and more lately, unfulfilled. But Mercia, no matter how much she needed warmth and friendship and fulfilment, would never accept it unless she married again.

"Mercy dear," her mother said. "We'd love some tea."

"I'll go and get it." Mercia sprang up, truly eager not to hear what she obviously felt was a confession, and her mother leaned across and rested a hand on Vanessa's. "How old is he?" she asked.

"Fifty-one," Vanessa told her.

"Vanessa, darling," her mother went on, "can he, will he, be able to marry you? If he can and will, then it may be worth waiting. If he can't, if you are thinking of being his mistress, you must be even more sure of yourself and of him than if you were going to get married."

Vanessa said: "She may not divorce him."

"Has he talked to her about it?"

"No," said Vanessa. "No, not yet."

"Have you tried to persuade him to?"

"No," answered Vanessa, quite sharply. She sounded shocked. "Would you expect me to?"

"No," said her mother, gently. "I would hope you

wouldn't, because I would hope he wouldn't need persuading. Vanessa, my darling, how much do you care?"

Vanessa, eyes painful from tears again, replied: "Sometimes it's nearly unbearable. Sometimes I hardly realise that there's any difficulty, it just seems a matter of time before we can be together."

"And you *know* that is what you want?"

"Yes," answered Vanessa simply. "I know."

"And what he wants?" her mother probed.

"I think I'm sure," Vanessa answered, and after a pause, went on: "Until you asked I had no doubt of it. I believe — I believe in him." After another pause, she added in a tone of finality: "Implicitly."

"Vanessa —" her mother began.

"Yes, darling?"

"Forgive me, but — do you sleep with him?"

Very directly, Vanessa answered: "Yes."

"How long have you known him?"

"Nearly a year. Mother, I couldn't tell you before. I — well, I couldn't."

"You told me when you had to," her mother said. "Darling, don't worry about me, or your father, or even Mercy, who may be very disapproving for a while. Your concern has to be for yourself. I may be able to show you some aspects which love has blinded you to, and if I know you there isn't much you've missed. Do you visit him at his home?"

"No," Vanessa said. "At the home of a friend. We meet by day."

"And the friend is away by day?"

"Yes."

"Is he — this man you love — rich or poor?"

"He's not rich like Daddy, but he's comfortably off," Vanessa said.

"What does he do?" asked her mother.

"He—he's of independent means."

"*No* profession?" For the first time her mother sounded almost disapproving.

"He trained as an accountant. He *is* an accountant." Vanessa was very quick in defence. "He does a great deal of work for various charities. He is on the Central Committee of World Food, for instance. He — he's *good*."

Her mother said: "Darling, I must find out all I can about him from you. I'm sorry if some questions hurt. Is he — a Don Juan, shall I say?"

"No," answered Vanessa. "At least —" She broke off with a twisted smile.

"You don't think so," her mother finished, lightly. "What is his background? Would your Aunt Jessamine approve, for instance?"

This time, Vanessa laughed. "She might give a sniff or two! Mummy, darling, he's quite acceptable in the commonly understood sense. Not that —"

"It would make any difference if he wasn't!"

"I don't really think that's true," replied Vanessa, thoughtfully. "I think I — well, I *don't* think I would be happy with anyone who didn't have the same standards as we have. I really don't. He —" Now she was nettled. "He was at Galeston and Christ's College, Oxford. He's lived all his life in the house his grandfather built, even if it was built of money made out of trade."

"What trade?" her mother asked.

"Machinery — farm machinery, farm implements, at first. *Does* it matter?" A tone of indignation was in Vanessa's voice.

"Only that I should be able to tell your father," Lady Belhampton said. "No, dear, it doesn't matter at all." She paused for a few moments, then stretched out both hands. "Have you met his wife?"

Vanessa took her mother's hands; and her own were cold.

"No," she said.

"Are there children?"

"Three — all grown up and away from home."

"So — she's alone."

Vanessa drew in a sharp breath.

"Must you say it like that?" she asked, thinly.

"Yes," her mother answered. "She would be alone if he left her, wouldn't she?"

"Yes," Vanessa made herself reply.

"Do you think he will be able to bring himself to leave her?" Lady Belhampton asked.

"I — yes. Yes, I think so."

"For you?"

"Mother — Mother, *must* you turn this into a cross-examination?" Vanessa pleaded.

"Yes," her mother replied quietly. "If I am to help."

"How *can* you help?"

"Well," Lady Belhampton said, "I could be wholly for you."

"I don't — I don't quite understand."

"Vanessa," her mother said, "if I am to be wholly for you, I must know all there is to know. If you are twenty years younger than his wife —"

"I'm not! She's forty-five."

"Much younger, then. If she has borne his children, if she has let herself go, let her looks go, her figure, then he might simply be tired of her because she's no longer attractive."

"She — she is a very beautiful woman," Vanessa stated simply.

"So you've seen her?"

"Only at a distance."

"Does he —" Lady Belhampton let Vanessa's hands go, in a gesture almost of disgust. "*He*. What is his name, darling?"

"Jacob Stone," said Vanessa.

"Does Jacob talk much about his wife?"

"Some — sometimes."

"When did she cease to be attractive to him?"

Vanessa answered: "He has been unhappy for much of the marriage. Most of it. Oh Mother, Mother. This *is* a cross-examination. It really is."

"Of course it is," said her mother gently. "Vanessa, my darling, I couldn't stand by and see you break up a man's home — no, don't be angry, listen to me — if I thought he were tired of a woman near his own age, and wanted a younger wife. It happens so often and it can be very, very cruel. *Vanessa, listen!* It would be quite different if I knew he had been unhappy, or half-happy, or never in love with his wife. That he had stayed until the children were grown up and gone, for their sake as much as hers. A human being needs some happiness. Often a man cannot find it with the woman whom he married long years ago. As often, a woman can't. If this man deserves happiness, if you can give it to him —"

"Oh, I can!" cried Vanessa.

"Why can't she?" her mother flashed.

This time, there was a long pause. In the distance there was a rattle of cups, so Mercia was on the way with the tea trolley. Vanessa had forgotten her until that moment, wished her far away now, as she sought desperately for the words she needed to explain. She had not known her mother in such a penetrating mood, never known such sharp and pointed questions since the small sins and the petty deceits of childhood.

At last, Vanessa said: "I think all she can hope to hold

him with is her body. I think she is maliciously possessive and by her possessiveness has made his life desperately unhappy."

Softly into the room's silence but as the rattling tray drew nearer, her mother asked gently:

"And what of her? Has she been happy? Or has he made her as desperately unhappy as he tells you she has made him? Vanessa, my darling, these are not just questions I am asking you; they are the questions you should surely be asking yourself. You know that. You *must* know that."

Chapter Four

THE GROWING HATE

Before I'll let him go to another woman, I'll kill him, Anne thought, with a fury close to venom. I'll kill him.

They were back in the house, going side by side up the stairs, as they had so often done before. He was evading her glances, and she was keeping up a kind of commentary: on the children, on Anthony in particular, the need for younger servants, the impossibility of running the house without them. The weather, friends, where they should go for a holiday. He responded with odd words and phrases, and she knew what was going on in his mind, knew what would happen when they reached the landing.

Unless she forced the issue.

Often, when they had been to swim, like this, and had come back to bath or shower, they had tumbled on to her bed, for so long their bed; somehow those twenty minutes of absolute ecstasy for her, and she had believed for him, had been the most treasured, partly because they had been stolen from the day. Now, he was going to his own room, either with an excuse or without a word.

They reached her door.

If she asked, invited, offered herself and he refused her, she would feel like hating him.

Jacob thought: how on earth can I say 'no'? How can I?

But if he went in with her, what then? When could he tell her the truth? He couldn't possibly make love to her, and go down to dinner, and wait until they were alone and tell her that he was in love with another woman and wanted a divorce. Yet he could not procrastinate any further; the radiance in Vanessa's eyes seemed to shine on him. He couldn't lie by word or deed any longer.

* * *

"Jacob," Anne said. "Come with me, darling."

Oh God, dear God, what shall I do if he refuses?

* * *

I can't go in and make love, not now, not again.

But oh God, what will happen if I refuse her?

* * *

They stood at the door of her room. Her smile, at first so natural, became set and artificial, for she knew that he really was going to make an excuse, and undoubtedly it was the worst insult she could suffer. She watched his growing pallor. She *knew* the agony that was going through his mind. And yet, if she lost now, she would have lost forever.

She stretched out a hand and touched him.

"Darling," she said. "Please."

Oh God! He groaned within himself. I can't — yet I can't turn away — I must —

Something inside him seemed to thrust words on to his tongue. He had not really meant to speak now, it was simply that her pleading made simple rejection impossible. Yet any course, except capitulation, would precipitate a scene. He had always fought against telling her because he could not face the expression that would grow on her face; the recrimination, the shouting, the screaming, the hysteria. Yet words were forced out of him, as if some unseen spirit was pushing them from his mind through to his lips.

His lips were so dry he could hardly form words; but he uttered her name.

"Anne —"

"Please, Jacob. Whatever is worrying you doesn't matter. I can — I can help you to forget it."

"Anne," he blurted, "there's something I must talk to you about."

It was almost as if desperation flared into her.

"No!" she exclaimed. "Not now, come and lie down, come —"

"*I tell you I must talk to you!*" he cried.

He did not know that he was shouting; he did not know that he was trembling. He saw her smile fade, saw her flinch. This time, she didn't speak, just watched him.

"I must speak to you," he said more quietly.

"All right, dear," she said. "Come in and talk."

* * *

She thought: if he refuses even to come into my room to talk, I — I — I'll *kill* him.

She knew that it was a wild thought, but she also knew it was how she felt. If he refused even to come and talk —

He moved past her.

The room, the loveliest in the house, had great bay windows overlooking the land on the southern side of King's Narrows. In the distance was the grey spire of the village church, the red roofs of the Elizabethan houses and cottages there. And trees. The room itself was in Regency period. There was a love seat in the bay windows, there was silver on the dressing-table, and French paintings on the walls. The colour motif was varied — silver and gold and green and yellows. The carpet was soft, one's feet sank into it.

"Jacob," Anne said. "Don't make yourself talk. There's no need to."

"I must," he insisted.

"You're not well, you're not yourself," she said, in a shriller voice. And she thought: *he mustn't tell me he's going to leave me. I can't stand it. I simply can't stand it!* "Shall I get you a drink? I've some sherry —"

"Anne," he said. "Sit down."

They were by the window now, and slowly she sat in the love seat, so that they were opposite each other, with the buttoned padding of the seat in between. She was trembling, while his face was chalk-white, his eyes strangely brilliant. Looking at her he could hardly control his lips, but at last he said:

"Anne, I hate to hurt you, but —"

Don't say it, for God's sake don't say it!

"But I — I would like — I want —"

Don't say it!

"Anne," he said. "I've fallen in love with another woman. I — I can't go on deceiving you. I can't go on."

Deceiving me? What makes him think he's ever deceived me? There was white-hot rage in her and yet there was also dread; she had heard but did not want to believe.

"Jacob, don't —" she managed to begin, but he would not stop.

"I've got to tell you," he muttered. "You've got to know." Somehow their hands were clutching, tight and hurtful. "I — I can't go on living here with you, Anne. I hate hurting you, but —"

She said, in a strangely cold way: "If you hate hurting me, why are you doing it?"

"Anne, I've fought against it —"

"It's nonsense," she interrupted in that same cold voice. "We've been married for twenty-five years. I've been faithful to you. I've given you three children. I've given you the best years of my life. I am yours," she went on with ruthless precision. "And you are *mine*. If you think I am ever going to let you go, you must have taken leave of your senses. Nothing would ever make me divorce you. Nothing in this world. So let's forget it. Let's forget you ever talked about it."

He heard each word as a blow. He should have known how she would react, but he had feared the outcry and the hysteria, not this blank refusal to think or even to consider.

* * *

Before I'll let him go, I'll kill him, she thought.

* * *

"Anne," he said. "I know it's a terrible shock, but —"

"It's not a shock at all. I've seen this coming for a long time. I hoped you would come to your senses before it became too serious, but obviously you haven't."

He said, sharply: "Oh, but I have."

"What do you mean?"

"I have come to my senses. I can't go on with you, Anne. I'll settle half of what I have on you. If — if you want this house then it's yours but —"

"*You fool!*" she screamed: and before he realised what she was going to do, she swung her arm and struck him savagely across the face, the expected hysteria bursting out like a volcano. "I'll never let you go. I'll see you dead first! I've given you everything, the best years of my life — *I won't let you go!*" Her voice was strident now, her mouth wide open, her eyes had a hot brilliance, her body was convulsed. "It's a wicked thing to do, only a bitch of a woman would make you do this, only a bitch would break up a happy marriage. That's what she is, she's a bitch, bitch, bitch..."

It was useless to try to quieten her.

He sat without moving, stunned, while the torrent poured out of her, the hurt, the hate, the venom, everything he had glimpsed in her over their years together, all he had seen and heard poured over their daughters' friends; half forgotten but now vividly remembered spasms of sheer hatred — and always, always followed by tears, by protestations of goodwill, by pleas for forgiveness gradually weakening until forgetfulness came and she forgot, or she pretended to forget. And in forgetting, she became a different person, soft and gentle and kind, incapable of saying what she had said, a stranger to spitting venom.

But now —

Her shrieks battered against his ears, unceasing.

He could not stay, it was impossible.

Some inner force had driven him to talk tonight, now the same inner force was driving him to get up and leave her. His body felt stiff, but he stood up. She was leaning forward and glaring at him, not shouting now, but sobbing.

"How could you do this to me how could you do this to me how could you be so cruel how could you do this to me..."

He saw the madness in her eyes and the alarming pallor of her face, the way her lips tightened until they seemed to have no shape at all. He turned away. He heard her rushing after him but did not turn to face her, nor did he quicken or slacken his pace. He thought that she might strike him, but instead she rushed past, reached the door and turning round blocked it, arms stretched so that she clutched both sides of the door frame.

Her face was distorted: like a hideous mask.

"*No!*" she screamed. "You mustn't leave me!"

Short of thrusting her aside he could not pass. He felt icy cold, and his heart was so heavy he did not think there could ever be light-heartedness again.

"No!" she cried, distraught. "Don't go! Please don't go. I didn't mean it. Oh God, I swear I didn't mean it. Please, please don't go."

But if he stayed tonight, then every time he tried to get away it would be as bad or even worse than this.

"Jacob," she gasped, letting her hands fall, and then stretching her arms towards him. "I didn't mean it. I didn't know what I was saying. I love you so much that the thought of losing you makes me insane. It drives me insane, I tell you." Now her arms were about him and she was trying to draw him close. "Please don't go. Not tonight, I couldn't stand it if you left me tonight. I won't — I won't carry on again like that, I swear I won't, only — *please don't go.*"

* * *

How could he leave her?

How could any man with a heart leave her?

How could he reject such pleading? How could he walk out on the woman he had known so long, when she pleaded like this?

How could he?

But if he stayed, how could he ever bring himself to say again that he would leave her?

* * *

She thought: He's going to stay. Oh, thank God, he's going to stay. I've won. Her arms were round his shoulders, and she felt his unyielding stiffness, she might have been a sack of wool, not warm and desirable flesh and blood. What could she say to keep him? What words would serve?

"Jacob," she said, "let's talk. I promise I'll be reasonable and calm, I won't let myself go again. I'll be dispassionate, I really will."

She thought: He's going to stay! She felt a flash of triumph but it did not last, for he didn't relax, and his lips began to move.

He asked: "Do you mean that?"

"Of course I mean it! Oh Jacob, let's discuss it calmly, like civilised people. It was such a shock I didn't know what I was saying or doing. Please promise you won't leave tonight."

He said: "I won't leave until we've talked, anyhow."

"Oh, bless you! Oh, that's wonderful. I — I won't be long, I'll just slip on a dress, we can have a drink before dinner. You — you *do* promise?" She stretched out to reach both sides of the door again. "Promise, Jacob."

"I won't go until we've talked," he said again, and he felt as if he were dying.

"Oh, thank God," she breathed. "I can't bear the thought of losing you. I don't think I could live without you. I love you so." Suddenly she moved forward and gripped his hands tightly, thrusting her face close to his so that her eyes seemed huge and glittering. "You do know I love you, don't you? You *do* know?"

He made a great effort, and at last answered:

"Yes, I know."

"I love you more than life itself," she cried, and then drew back and spun round and out of sight, leaving him alone.

Alone. It was like being in the utter stillness that follows a storm. Unnatural. Unreal. He was keyed up for her to come back, for the screaming to begin again. But it did not. He turned to his bedroom and went in, closed the door with a light click, and then, feeling faint, feeling ill, he dropped on to the foot of his bed and sat absolutely still. After a while, he realised that his heart was thumping with a slow, relentless beat. It was painful, but soon it eased. He must get up. He must bath, that would relax him. Bath slowly; dress slowly, and then go downstairs.

To calm discussion? His mind rejected the very idea. It would not, could not be. He wondered whether he should break his promise and go. Now.

Chapter Five

DISCUSSION

Dulcie brought in the roast lamb, as always in these days of servant famine; she placed everything on the two hot-plates on the sideboard, and withdrew. Jacob carved with precise efficiency; Anne served the vegetables from modern cook-and-serve tureens. If Dulcie had heard anything of Anne's outburst, she showed no sign. Anne, dressed in a simple, sleeveless dress of pale blue, with a wide gilt belt, a little young for her age, sat opposite him at a small table. She looked not only too young, but too demure. There was a little tell-tale redness at her eyes which was hardly noticeable. Between them was a carafe of white wine and a similar carafe of red, some iced water and bread and butter. There was constraint between them but no tension.

Suddenly, as they began to eat, Anne said: "I am sorry, darling. Really I am."

"I'm surprised you didn't break my neck!" Jacob forced himself into a kind of jocularity which he hoped struck the right note.

"I think I nearly did," said Anne. "Darling, *are* you really serious? About the — this other woman, I mean."

With an even greater effort, Jacob said: "Yes, Anne, I'm afraid I am."

"But — but why? What have I done wrong?"

"It isn't a question of what either of us have done wrong —"

She flashed: "Most people would say you have."

He must still be careful, he realised, very careful indeed; rage, hysteria, were still very close to the surface. If he could possibly avoid saying the wrong thing — oh, that was idiotic, whatever he said would be wrong. It was like picking one's way over a patch of broken glass, fearful of a stab of pain at every step.

"Yes," he conceded. "I suppose they would."

"And you know it's wrong, don't you?" she accused.

"Anne," he said, "what are we going to have? A sensible discussion on the situation and what we should do — or a discussion on moral issues, which will get us nowhere?"

"Surely the two are inseparable."

"No," Jacob said. "They're not inseparable." When she didn't interrupt, he went on: "Anne, I know it sounds weak and pointless to say that I'm sorry, desperately sorry, to hurt you, but it's true."

She kept silent, this time.

"But there isn't any way of avoiding it," he went on.

She retorted sharply: "Yes there is. Give up this woman you imagine you're in love with. Come to your senses. If you'll forget it, I will."

The food which he was trying to eat was choking him. He should have known better than to attempt to reason with her; it wasn't fair on her or on him. He should have known that with Anne the only way to avoid scenes and recrimination and the gaping wounds of white-hot quarrelling was to walk out. And yet — twenty-five years. How could he simply turn his back?

"Anne," he said, "we are in a situation which is

familiar both to men and to women. I am in love with another woman, and —" he caught his breath at the sight of Anne's expression, but forced himself to go on "— and I want to marry her." He saw how she clenched her hands on knife and fork, realised how she was gritting her teeth, but went on: "It isn't any use staying in a marriage when there's not — not a hope of happiness for one of the two involved. God knows I wish it weren't so, but —" he gulped "— but I am telling you the truth."

"All right," she said tautly, "I will tell *you* the truth. Nothing will make me divorce you. Nothing. You may as well save your breath."

"Anne," he said, heavily, "it's no use talking like that. There's a new law, remember. After three years I can divorce you. All you could do is postpone the inevitable, and that wouldn't help either of us." When she didn't answer but, for the first time, looked shocked and shaken, he went on: "Can't we try to be objective? I will make a generous settlement on you. And as I've said, if you really want to go on living here, I will make the house over to you. Money won't —"

"You can't buy me," she interrupted, harshly.

"I'm not trying to buy you."

"I don't know what else you'd call it. Twenty-five years, the best years of my life, and you talk about money. Jacob, understand this once and for all: I shall never divorce you. And if you think this — this — this creature you're supposed to be in love with will wait three years, you're fooling yourself. All she wants is your money and your house and position; she can't fool me even if she fools you. She's no better than those hippies camping in King's Narrows, sprawling all over one another — it's like a farmyard. We might be living in a permissive society but I'm not giving way to it. The answer is *no*, Jacob. I shall never divorce you."

* * *

He thought: she means it. The strange thing was that although he was so bitterly resentful, that although he could look back over the years with little recollection of happiness, he could feel sorry for her. He did feel sorry. He saw more clearly than he had seen before that she was indeed stripped of everything but him, and that she would fight for him to the very last ditch.

Nothing was going to be easy.

And there was Vanessa, who hoped for so much.

And he, who longed for Vanessa.

All he could do was make Anne understand that he was immovable. But it was tearing her apart, and instead of getting better, it would get worse for her.

How could he help? Was there any way at all?

* * *

Anne thought: he's bound to come to his senses. He's bound to. All I've got to do is to be nice to him. Understanding. Forgiving. Oh God, give me the strength to be patient, because I hate her so.

I must be understanding.

I must be forgiving.

I can't let him go: I would kill him first.

"Darling," she said. "I'm sorry I behaved as I did."

Sorry, sorry, sorry, she was always sorry.

"I am sorry about the situation, too," he said. "Desperately."

"Do you — do you really love this — this girl?"

"Yes, Anne."

"It isn't a passing fancy?"

"You know I wouldn't have talked to you as I have if it were."

"Is she — is she much younger than I?"

"A bit," he admitted.

"How much?"

"She's in the early thirties."

"Oh," exclaimed Anne. "You *are* baby-snatching. More coffee?"

They were in the front room, with its Regency elegance, sitting in a window seat and watching the fading afterglow, the softness of dusk on every hand, the deep purples and blues, where there had been greens and browns. The drive wound between grass-clad banks with shrubs and trees in full leaf. Now and again, beyond the trees, the headlights of a car showed. They had been here for fifteen minutes or so, sitting quietly. They had finished the meal quietly, too. Now, she talked without venom, as if in simple curiosity.

He didn't respond to the 'baby-snatching'; just shrugged.

"Is she attractive?" Anne asked.

"I think so."

"A beauty?"

"Some would say she was."

"Does she live near here?"

"In London."

"Has she ever been married?"

"No."

"Why not?" asked Anne, more sharply. But she smiled as she handed him more coffee and there was still no hint of a return to the hysterical mood.

"I — I don't know," he said.

"If she's thirty-one or two and beautiful she must have had *affaires*." When he didn't answer, Anne went on:

"Are you one of her *affaires*? Or don't you know?" When he still didn't answer, she went on in a very quiet, dogged-sounding voice: "Do you know I've never looked at another man? I've been absolutely faithful to you since we were married, long before we were married, as a matter of fact. Did you know that? Jacob! Answer me! Did you know that?"

He knew, or at least he felt sure, that it was absolutely true. Never had he wished it were not so, but there she sat, peering at him, demanding an answer. She *was* beautiful. She *was* sexually attractive. A hundred men might lose their heads over her, but there she was demanding an answer, and he could guess what would follow as he said:

"Yes, I know."

"Then why do you want to leave me?"

"Anne," he said, "you know why."

How could he tell her that he had longed to, so often? How could he tell her that by pretending to be in love with her, or at least to love her, he had lived a lie? How could he cause even more hurt than he had already? He put his cup down. It was useless to go on; there had to be an end to this ceaseless argument, and he would have to make the end. But as he started to rise she put a hand on his knee.

"Don't go, Jacob. I promise not to talk about it any more tonight."

She might mean that, but could she restrain herself for more than a few minutes?

"Let's sleep on it," she went on, with brittle brightness. "Perhaps there's something on television we might watch, or — or we could go for a walk or for a drive or just sit. I won't talk about it any more, Jacob. Honestly."

And she did not.

It was a strange evening, spent together until he went

to his study. It was eleven o'clock when he went upstairs. He looked into her room, where the door was open; she was sitting on the love seat, surrounded by letters, and he knew they were his — to her. Love letters. Oh, dear God, why had he lied to her?

She was in tears; quietly, undemonstratively. He said 'Goodnight' and all she did was to rest her head back on a cushion and let the tears fall. "Goodnight," he repeated and went out. He felt an awful burden, of guilt, of a kind of shame, of responsibility spurned. It didn't matter how he tried to evade the responsibility or excuse himself, he *had* caused this. The price of his happiness was Anne's misery. And he knew, he needed no telling that she would stay like this for a long, long time. It wasn't only bitterness at being scorned. It wasn't only jealousy. It wasn't only a sense of loss: it was pain. He stood at his window looking on to distant lights, and the deep red glow over London. He walked about, too restless to get undressed. He kept seeing Vanessa's face and hearing her laugh and feeling her touch, but she was far away, remote, and the tear-dazed woman, the stranger he had lived with all these years, sat as if stricken in the next room.

* * *

She said, aloud: "I'll kill him rather than let him go."

* * *

He went out of the room and down the stairs and out into the grounds. There were pale paths which guided him although he walked on the lush grass which was springy under his heels. From King's Narrows came the sound of guitar music and singing, so out of place here. Many of the people in the new houses were petitioning the police to move the little colony on, but they did no harm, and they had their own concepts of right and wrong and happiness. He walked at speed, not thinking, just feeling. Vanessa was nearer when he was out-of-doors, and he needed her. He needed to touch and to talk to her, but he could not touch and, unless he telephoned, he could not speak to her. In any case, what right had he to call her, now? She would hear the distress in his voice, he would have to tell her what had caused it, and he knew what she would say.

"Jacob, we can't go on."

He had led her to believe, or at least strongly to hope, that Anne would take the news well. It had been a kind of lie. The kind of lie, if he faced the facts, that he had used all his life with Anne.

Why couldn't he tell her the truth?

Why couldn't he go now and telephone Vanessa? Why couldn't, why didn't he get out his car and drive to see her? It wasn't eleven yet, there were a dozen places where they could meet and talk. The temptation was almost overwhelming, but he fought it back, knowing that to see Vanessa, upset as he was, could only unsettle her and fill her with doubts.

But if that were true, it meant that he did not, could not trust her absolutely.

He paced on, agitated not only by what had happened between him and Anne but by his apprehensions about Vanessa. What would she do if she knew that Anne would make them wait for at least the three years demanded by the law? He couldn't guess. He could hope and believe but couldn't possibly be sure. But he was sure that he would have to be in a far calmer, confident mood than this.

He reached the pool.

The only light came from the stars; and the reflection of the stars. The only sound from the hippies and distant cars and near-by rustling among trees and bushes. He stood by the edge of the pool, near the spot where he had dived in this afternoon. He saw so much on the mirror of his mind, and all so vivid. There was a gentle breeze which made the pool's surface ripple. There were the ghost-like voices of the children. There was all his life, going through his mind, the hesitations, and the fears, the knowledge — yes, the knowledge of the misery of the past twenty-five years. He *had* hated them. He could so vividly recall standing here one windy day and looking at the whipping waves. There had been a kind of quarrel. Anne had savaged Joan about her love for a boy, accusing her of sleeping with him, with anyone who attracted her. And she had spun round on him and rasped in venom:

"*You* ought to be talking to her, she's your daughter as well as mine. *You* ought to tell her that no daughter of ours is going to sleep around like a whore. *You* tell her, instead of leaving all the dirty work to me."

And Joan, so young, so fair, so hurt, so pale, had simply looked at him with tear-touched eyes.

"Joan," he had said, "your mother is upset. I know she trusts you as much as I do."

Joan, tears spilling now, had walked away. And Anne, hardly able to believe that he would defy her so, had raged about his craven permissiveness; spat that if Joan, if any of the children 'went wrong' then he and only he would be to blame.

"I don't know who's to blame," he had said. "But never let me hear you talk to Joan or to Angela like that again."

Now, they were both married; happily married. But how heavy his heart had been that night and for so many nights thereafter; how utterly despairing he had felt because there was no hope of understanding between his wife and him. It had been hopeless for many years before that; hopeless, then. And it was the same now, except that there was the golden promise for him.

He half-turned.

He heard a different sound; of footsteps, very close. He turned to the right, and saw Anne, head swathed in a white scarf, Anne with an arm raised and something in it; Anne, striking him with awful violence on the side of the head, sending him staggering, aware only of pain.

Then he fell into the pool and the water closed over him.

Chapter Six

NEAR DEATH

He didn't lose consciousness.

He was aware of both pain and of the acute danger that he might drown.

He saw the past and he saw the moment when Anne had struck him; like an endless sequence of photographs flashing in front of his eyes he saw all that had happened between them. All those things which had been tormenting him and haunting him, all those things he had been attempting to recall, all those moments when he had come close to hating her, those when he had feared her for the violence she might do: all these were shown him with terrifying vividness.

The rage which could spring, on the instant, to her face.

The tightening at her lips, which could be the prelude to spitting venom.

The smiles which could follow: the 'I am sorry, my darling', which was at once truth and lie; the contrite 'I did not realise what I was doing' — the change which came, like crocodile tears, the moment she realised that she had won whatever she wanted at the moment, or else, more seldom, when she knew she had not won but in fact might lose for good if she forced the issue at that moment.

The whole misery; the despair; the holding on to 'save' the marriage, or for the children, or because it would inevitably hurt her; all these things were revealed to him so that now he had no doubt at all: he was right to leave her, and must go.

But he was drowning.

He could feel weight and pressure at his chest and water in his mouth and at his eyes. He was drowning.

But he was alive.

Don't struggle, he thought in reflex, don't struggle. Float to the surface. *Swim* to the surface. He made two breast strokes, and then realised that he did not know whether he was heading upwards or downwards or sideways, or —

He broke surface.

He began to gasp for breath. He began to cough and choke but contrived, not knowing how, to keep his head above the water. Then his right arm touched the side of the pool, and he knew that he was safe. He clutched the rail with his hand, having the sense to rest and not yet to try to pull himself up. He floated. He coughed and spluttered until the water was gone from his mouth and, he thought, from his lungs. He raised his other hand until he was holding on by both. And for the first time he opened his eyes, wide.

There were the distant stars, and nearer, between the trees, lights of houses. There was a shaft of brilliance as a car drove with its headlights showing the outline of the trees, of bushes, of small sheds, even of tents in King's Narrows. Slowly, he turned in the other direction: and he saw the house — King's House. His house. Lights were shining, all of them upstairs. He did not realise at first from which windows, he was still so dazed, but there was the house standing, firm and massive: his house, his home.

The corner light was from her room: Anne's room.

The one on the left was his. And there was the landing light, always left on at night.

He saw a shadowy movement at Anne's window: *Anne.*

She stood there. He could see only the outline, not the face, but he knew it too well to have any doubts.

"My God!" he exclaimed aloud. "The cold-blooded bitch!"

And so she was. She had struck and toppled him into the pool and left him to drown. He was thinking swiftly, now. It could not be five minutes since she had struck him. Five? Four? Six? She must have seen him go under and then hurried to the house, losing no time.

My God, he thought, she tried to murder me!

He began to shiver, aware that his head was aching violently. But he was shocked into action and, hand over hand, moved towards the head of the pool. He rested for a few moments, then groped for the steps with his left foot, found it, and slowly climbed on to them. At the top, his clothes heavy with dripping water, he swayed; and for a horrified moment feared that he would fall back into the pool. He lurched forward, taking a few staggering steps, until the danger was past.

Anne had gone from the window, and the blind was down; it was as if she had sent him out of her life.

The cold-blooded —

"I could choke the life out of her," he rasped. "I could choke the life out of her."

And in that moment, how he wanted to!

He reached the front of the house, then stopped, abruptly. The door was closed. If she had locked and bolted it, how could he get in? He pushed, and the door did not budge. He put his right hand to his pocket and groped among small silver for his keys. He found the door key and groped for the keyhole. If she had locked and bolted it —

The key turned, the door gave way and opened wide. A dim light glowed from the landing. He closed the door, then groped his way towards the downstairs cloakroom. He began to peel off his clothes. Clammy and cold, they clung to his body. He set the shower to medium, then stepped inside. The water fell gently, softly, warming, until his shivering ceased and thought returned; but all he could think about was Anne and what she had set out to do.

She had meant to *murder* him.

He turned the shower off and, as he groped for a towel, saw his reflection in the mirror. He expected to see blood from his temple, but there was none. There was redness and swelling, but no bleeding. He dabbed his hair gingerly and then sat on a low stool and dried himself all over. He felt much better; warmer; free from shock except at recollection. Yes, now, it *was* recollection: as of something which had happened in the past which had come before him in those vivid flashes.

But there were his sodden clothes; and there was a pool of water, seeping from them. He picked up the trousers and put his right hand to the pocket, taking out the keys and some silver and the wallet from the hip pocket. All movements were difficult and everything stuck to his fingers and hands.

He hung the trousers and jacket on a hook, and went out. Apart from the drip, drip, drip behind him, there was no sound until he reached the hall. From there the ticking of the grandfather clock was audible. It accompanied him up the stairs, fading slowly. A large mirror filled a wall at the half-landing and he was startled by the sudden apparition of his naked figure, his right hand clutching the oddments. He almost sniggered.

He reached the main landing. His own door, near him, was open; Anne's, at the far end, was closed.

He felt a sudden fury of rage. That she could do such a thing! That she could come from behind him and strike him, leaving him to drown.

He forced himself to turn into his own room and began to move very quickly, doing commonplace things with a restrained violence. Pyjamas *on*, jacket *on*, slippers *on*: on! He strode into his bathroom. Toothbrush — *snatch*. Toothpaste — *grab*. He spun the cap off and paste oozed out. "Bloody thing!" he growled, but he brushed his teeth, hurting his gums. *Rinse, rinse!* He spun round from the hand basin and caught the side of his head against the bathroom cabinet which he hadn't quite closed. "*God!*" he gasped, and pain seared through him. After a few moments the pain eased, and he closed the door carefully.

Suddenly, he started: for he could see his reflection in the cabinet mirror, and blood was seeping down his face.

After the first shock he begun to laugh. The laughter grew — not louder but inwardly, until it began to choke him and also to make his temple throb with almost unbearable pain. He must keep still. He stood absolutely still and the pain eased. He made his way back to the bedroom. He needed a drink, of course, but he didn't keep liquor up here. Anne did! Whisky, gin, sherry, and what she called 'the fixings'. But he couldn't go into her room, the sight of her would goad him to violence.

She — had — actually — tried — to — murder — him.

She — had — gone — off — leaving — him — for — dead.

It was incredible; unthinkable; unreal; and yet it had happened; it was a fact. He clenched his teeth against the rising anger. Words surged into his mind. He wanted a drink. Drink. Not downstairs. Head throbbed too much. Drink. Anne's room. *No.* Mustn't go in there. *Must — not — go — in — there.* The sight of her sleeping or pretending to be asleep would be too much. ***Drink.***

Ah! Tea!

What was the matter with him? Some tea would be good,

just what he wanted, and he could make his own. There was an electric kettle, tea, milk, sugar, in a cabinet here as well as in Anne's room, so that they could make their own tea without calling Dulcie, or any second maid they happened to employ at any given time.

Tea.

These simple actions helped and soothed him. As he waited for the kettle to boil he actually looked through *The Times*. He read but did not take in the news of daily happenings. The pictures of politicians and sportsmen. It was all remote. He was remote. This was a kind of dream. Nightmare. The kettle boiled and he made the tea. There was a tin of chocolate biscuits. He munched some, drank tea, and every now and again had to make himself admit the truth: that Anne, in the next room, had tried to kill him and thought him dead, because he wanted to leave her: *because he loved Vanessa.*

The tea was good; the biscuits, too.

He munched and thought: What shall I do?

He could go in and accuse Anne, though not at the moment, for he would find it almost impossible to keep his hands away from her. Even at the thought of seeing her his whole body began to tense. But how could he behave as if it hadn't happened? How could he go to bed? God! What a shock she would get in the morning when she found he was alive!

Nonsense: he couldn't go to bed as if nothing had happened.

He could pack some clothes and leave.

That would probably be the best thing. It was only a matter of time now, there wasn't the slightest doubt that he must go. Why not take this chance? The idea became more attractive the more he thought about it. He had only to put a few clothes in a suitcase and in a hanging bag, go downstairs, get the car out and drive off. It wasn't late yet — what time *was* it? He glanced at the clock on his bed-side table, and exclaimed:

"Only twenty to twelve!"

It seemed as if it were the middle of the night.

Yes — he must go. No more scenes, no more conflict, once he was away the worst of the trouble would be over. Once Anne woke to find him gone she would realise there was no hope, she would accept the situation as it was.

She would have to.

He knew she had tried to murder him and sooner or later he would tell her so. "Let's have no more nonsense, Anne: we don't want the world to know that you attempted to murder me. And you must know as well as I do that it's all over between us: there never was any hope."

He must go.

She would be terrified of the truth coming out.

A spasm of a new kind of fear shot through him. She would be terrified, she would do anything to conceal it, but then, so would he. The last thing he would want was Vanessa to know. If Vanessa thought that Anne had been driven to such desperate straits, would she go on with him? Even if he were free would she marry him?

He did not know.

He was beginning to sweat. He must see Vanessa and talk to her. Whatever happened, she had to know the whole truth. If he began to keep things from her now it would prey on his mind and there could be no full trust between them. He ought to telephone Vanessa this minute and tell her he was coming; before this night was out he must talk to her, for the shadow of fear, that when she knew how desperately Anne felt she would not go on with it, haunted him.

"*The one thing that really worries me, Jacob, is the thought of breaking up a home, trying to build happiness on another woman's broken marriage.*"

At the time, he had tried to reassure her. In fact he had not wanted to face the truth; he had deceived himself as he had throughout the marriage, into believing, into wishful thinking, that Anne would behave differently; reasonably.

What a bloody fool he had been! And what a bloody fool he still was!

He must not build another fool's paradise. He had to talk to someone, and who better than the woman he so loved? And if he had fears of how she would respond, then when better to find out?

He moved abruptly from his chair and snatched up the telephone by the side of it.

There was no buzzing sound; it was dead.

It took him seconds to realise this, to feel an almost childish rage. This was an extension from the main instrument downstairs, there was another in Anne's room, and when that was through to her, it was cut off from him, and vice versa. The control switch was in her room, which had once been theirs. He held the instrument so tightly that his knuckles went white, then slowly relaxed. The only way to use the telephone now was to switch through from her room: then it would be usable both here and downstairs.

So he had to go out to telephone, or go into Anne's room.

He hesitated for what seemed a long time, then went out and to her door. He gripped the handle and turned slowly. He need only switch the instrument, it would make hardly any sound and if she were asleep, it wouldn't wake her.

The cold-hearted bitch!

He gritted his teeth to try to keep back his rage, and opened the door.

The bedside light was on.

He saw this and saw Anne but on that first instant did not realise what had happened, and he stood staring. She was propped up on pillows, with her head lolling on her chest, so that he could not see her face. But he could see the open, empty bottle by her side, and the glass with a little water in it, and the stillness of her body. And as he rushed across the room, calling: "Anne!" in a muted voice, he realised exactly what had happened.

After leaving him for dead, she had come back here and taken an overdose of sleeping pills, intending to kill herself.

Chapter Seven

TO LET HER DIE?

"Anne," Jacob called again. "Anne."

His voice was husky and low-pitched, partly from the shock. She did not stir. He reached her and placed his hands on her shoulders so as to raise her head. Her eyes were closed, her lips slack, she hardly seemed to be breathing.

"*Anne!*" he rasped.

But he could not wake her, and he knew it. He was not sure that she still lived. He was aware of no thoughts except about her stillness and whether she was alive. He put his head to her heart, feeling the warmth and weight of her breast, and could detect a little beating, very faint; *very* faint, but none the less it was beating. He drew back, letting her head droop again.

If he left her here she would die.

There were other thoughts in his mind: positive thoughts. She often slept badly. She often had sleeping tablets. Sean McNamara, their friend and doctor, had recently given her some very strong tablets, adding the warning: "Never more than two a night now." They had been downstairs, and Sean had been relaxing on his last call of the day, with a brandy. "See that she sticks to that, Jacob."

"I will."

And Anne had flashed: "Don't tell me you're going to start sleeping with me again, darling, to make sure I don't take an overdose."

With anyone else it could have been an embarrassing moment; with Sean it had been easy to laugh off. But at the door, when he had been alone with Sean, their friend had said:

"I mean it about those tablets, Jacob."

"I don't think you need worry," Jacob had said.

Now, he stood and stared at the bottle. He had no idea how many tablets she had taken, had no idea how many would be fatal, but he did not doubt that she had meant to take enough to kill herself: murder, and suicide.

A new thought fluttered close: this is where he had brought her; this was where their lives had led.

And — she would die.

He could leave her to die.

No one need know he had been in here. He had touched nothing but Anne herself, there could be no evidence. All he had to do was to turn round, go out, go down to the car — no: pack a few things first, then go down to the car, drive to London — he didn't even have to see Vanessa. He could leave a note here: that was it! He could leave a note for Anne, telling her he had left her, telling her to write to his club. No one would dream he had been here.

He stood, these thoughts flashing, seeing Anne's marble stillness. Perhaps a minute passed. Then, sudden and unexpected as the blow on his head, came a revulsion of feeling: he could not do this, it would be like committing murder. The change started in his mind and ran through his body; he could feel it physically. Then he plucked up the telephone, put it to his ear, heard the dialling tone and dialled with great precision. Soon, he could hear the ringing sound in Sean McNamara's house. He could picture it, one of the old houses in the village, low-ceilinged, oak-beamed, and always a little untidy, for what one child of Sean's seven didn't drop on the floor, another did. It was such a strange household, for only a year ago Sean's wife had died. Now his sister Eileen was foster-mother and house-keeper.

Could they all be out? Not everyone, surely. He became anxious, almost panic-stricken.

The ringing stopped, and Eileen answered in a far-away voice:

"Dr. McNamara's house."

"Eileen," said Jacob, without announcing himself. "Can Sean come over, right away?"

"Who — oh! Jacob." There was a very short pause and then in an almost hopeless tone, she went on: "Jacob, *must* he? He's only been in for half an hour, and he's tired out. Janice used to tell me how he worked but I didn't dream it was like this."

"It's absolutely vital," Jacob said. "I wouldn't drag him out if it weren't."

"All right, I —" There was a break in Eileen's voice, and: "He's here."

A moment later Sean's deep voice with its undertone of Dublin accent came on the line.

"Jacob, what's the matter?" He managed always to put a note of concern into his voice. Everyone trusted Dr. Mac, for whenever he was with them he made them feel there was no one else in the world.

Quietly, Jacob stated: "Anne's taken an overdose of those sleeping tablets you gave her."

"Has she, then! Do you know how many she's taken?"

"I don't know how many were in the bottle, but it's empty."

"How long ago?"

"An hour, perhaps."

"So she's well under. Jacob, I'll have to get her to hospital. I'll send an ambulance out at once, and I'll be there myself in a few minutes. Pile clothes on her, while you're waiting. Is Dulcie up?"

"No."

"Get a few things together," Sean said. "Change of nightdress, toothbrush — you know."

"Yes. Thank you, Sean."

"Yes," said Sean, vaguely, and before he rang off Jacob heard him saying to Eileen: "Call the hospital..." Then the line went dead and Jacob was alone in the silent room, staring at his wife. He drew up the bedclothes and tucked them round her shoulders. He thought her face was very cold. Nonsense! There hadn't been time for her to start going cold with rigor mortis. She looked dead, though. He felt utterly devoid of feeling, now that he had done what he should.

He ought to call Dulcie. She would hear the cars and lie wondering and worrying. He went out, casting a glance over his shoulder at Anne, whose head still drooped. There was another flight of six steps up the the half-floor where Dulcie had her room and where the children had slept once they were out of the nursery. A light was on in her room, showing beneath the door. He called:

"Dulcie, are you awake?"

Immediately there was a response: "Yes, sir. Is anything the matter?" And then she added: "Come in, please come in." He opened the door, to find her sitting up, a book on her lap, the bedside light on. Oddly, she looked younger; and he noticed that she read without glasses; at least, she wore none now.

"What is it, Mr. Jacob?" She was anxious.

"Mrs. Anne's taken too many sleeping tablets," he

answered simply. "Dr. McNamara is on his way, and an ambulance is, too. I thought you should know."

"Oh, my goodness," she said. "My goodness."

The strange thing was that she didn't seem surprised, and as he realised that, Jacob realised also that Sean hadn't, either. Sean had not made a single comment of any kind. For a moment he stared at this old woman who had know him most of his life, and it was she who broke the silence.

"Are you all right, sir?"

"Yes, Dulcie. It was a shock when I found her, but I'm all right now."

Then Dulcie said a strange thing, the full force of which didn't catch up with him until later. She looked at him with great intensity, her brow eyes huge and luminous, and stretched out a hand, so thin and bony.

"Whatever you do, Master Jacob," she said, "don't blame yourself." There followed a long silence as if she were trying desperately to make him realise how important that exhortation was; then at last she drew her hands back and went on: "I'll be along in a few moments, sir. Did the doctor say what to do?"

"Just keep her warm until he comes."

Dulcie nodded as if with complete understanding. Soon, she was in the room, and wrapping a winter-weight eiderdown about Anne, who still hadn't shifted her position. She caught the empty bottle with a corner of the eiderdown, and he shot a hand out to save it from falling, but it struck the base of the telephone sharply, making the instrument give a sharp ring, and did not fall.

"Stay with her," he said. "I'll open the front door."

"The quicker they come," she said, "the better."

He went down the stairs, putting on all the lights. He opened the front door and stepped on to the porch, looking along the drive. He had been there only a few seconds when headlights showed a car swinging off the road. Soon they played a kind of hide-and-seek among the trees, then they shone on Jacob and the house. The car passed the porch and pulled up beyond, and as it stopped the lights were switched off, and Sean climbed out. He was a short, thickset man, until recently a regular member of his Old Boys' rugby team, athletic, solid, utterly dependable. He came, his case swinging in an indication of his vigour.

"Is there any change?" he asked; and suddenly they were gripping hands.

"No. Dulcie's with her," Jacob told him.

"Good. Will you stay down and let the ambulance men in?"

"Yes, of course."

"We'll soon have her away," Sean promised, and he went into the house with his powerful, purposeful stride, and up the stairs, almost as familiar with this house as he was with his own. His footsteps made little sound. The feel of his grip lingered on Jacob's hand. Still no comment, Jacob reflected; it was almost as if he had expected something like this, or, at least, that he was not surprised.

Soon the ambulance turned into the drive, and from that moment much happened at great speed. Two ambulance men got out, the driver stayed at the wheel, moving the vehicle to an easier position when the men had gone in. Jacob showed them the way. Sean called out to them. Dulcie appeared at the landing, looking down. Almost as soon as they had gone into Anne's room, it seemed, they were out again, carrying her on a stretcher. They seemed oblivious of Jacob, who watched Anne's face, first in bright light and then in shadow, until she disappeared. The rumble of Sean's voice sounded, then his footsteps as he came down. He was solid and ruggedly good-looking, with his grey-streaked mane of hair, and his air of utter dependability.

They met halfway across the hall.

"Well?" Jacob asked.

"I don't know what will happen," Sean said. "Those damned things break up quickly, and get into the bloodstream. That's why they're so effective. But a stomach pump will help, and I've given her some shots. What can be done will be done." He stood quite still. "How long did it take you to call me, Jacob?"

Jacob said: "Perhaps two minutes."

"Jacob, I have to say this: she could die. And if she does, the police will want to know all the details, including details of any delays."

Dry-mouthed, Jacob said: "Yes." He nearly added: "You sound as if you think I've something to keep back." In fact, he simply added: "Of course."

"I'll come back as soon as I can," Sean promised, "but it may not be for several hours."

"I'll be here." Jacob tried to speak almost lightly; casually, but Sean McNamara did not take anything lightly tonight. His eyes, grey-green, were very bright, not so much accusing as demanding. "Sean," Jacob said. "What's the matter?"

"I'd like you to sleep," Sean said quietly.

"Good God, I can't go off to sleep! I must come to the hospital — what on earth am I thinking of?"

"I've given Dulcie some tablets for you," Sean said. "Take them with some warm milk, and then go to bed. You can't do anything useful by coming to the hospital, and you will be in far better shape if you get a few hours' sleep. Don't be stubborn, Jacob, please."

Jacob thought: He is hostile. He had never known Sean

in such a mood and neither liked nor understood it. There still had not been a single question or comment, just a calm acceptance of what had happened. Perhaps, now, there was a touch of impatience about him as he shifted from one foot to the other.

"Jacob —"

"Sean," Jacob said, abruptly, "do you see that?" He turned his head, to show the little scratch and the bruise, and for the first time Sean looked startled. He also looked at the bruise intently.

"What is it?"

"Anne struck me across the head tonight when I was standing by the pool. Look." He gripped Sean's wrist and led him towards the cloakroom. There were the sodden jacket and trousers, hanging; the other clothes on the floor in a pool of water. "She came back here, thinking I was dead, and took the sleeping tablets." He saw the expression change on Sean's face, for the first time tonight he saw concern. "Do you still think I should sleep it off?" he demanded roughly.

"What led up to such a situation?" Sean asked with obviously forced calm.

"We quarrelled," Jacob answered flatly.

"About your woman friend?"

It was pointless to ask 'how had he known?'; pointless to do anything but answer the question flatly:

"I'd asked her for a divorce. Yes."

He thought then: Sean's a Catholic. He wondered whether this explained his mood and his earlier attitude.

"So it's gone as far as that?" Sean gripped Jacob's hand tightly. "If she comes round we have a lot to talk about. If she doesn't —" He broke off. "Yes," he said, "I think you should sleep. I really do. Take those pills, Jacob, and that milk. Lying awake, going over it in your mind time and time again, won't help. Whichever way this goes, you've a lot to face up to in the morning. Be advised. If not by me, then by Dulcie. I *must* go. The ambulance will be at the hospital by now." He gave a final squeeze and then turned and strode off.

Jacob waited on the porch until the tail-light, a red eye, disappeared along the drive. Then he locked up and went upstairs. Of course, Dulcie was there, tablets on a saucer, warm milk in a glass, not smiling, but somehow reassuring: calming.

"The doctor said you should have this, Master Jacob."

"Don't you think I should be at the hospital?" asked Jacob.

"No, sir," she answered. "I think you need rest. Please do what he says, and — and try not to worry, sir. Try not to worry."

She was very close to tears.

Jacob got into bed and took the tablets and milk, and snuggled down, telling himself it was an incredible thing to do: but soon he found himself drifting and before long he was asleep.

* * *

Fifteen miles away, Vanessa slept; and now and again, she smiled.

Close at home, Dulcie tossed and turned, sleeping only fitfully.

At her home, Eileen McNamara slept in that catnap way she had become used to, whenever Sean was out at night. He worked so hard and was so tired most of the time, she always wanted to wake the moment he came in, to get anything he wanted. His wife had been the same.

The children slept soundly.

Sean McNamara did not sleep but, with a younger

doctor, a Pakistani of great understanding, worked to save Anne Stone from dying. There were moments during the night when they thought it was quite hopeless, when Sean himself believed that she would die and wondered bleakly what her death would mean to Jacob; how soon he would begin to blame himself.

Even by dawn, there was no certainty that Anne would live.

Chapter Eight

MORNING

A hand was on his shoulder, a man's voice in his ear. "Jacob, wake up." The hand pressed more firmly, the voice became louder, closer. Through the vagueness of waking, Jacob had a sense of alarm, and then suddenly recollection flashed into his mind and fear drove him to jerk upright in the bed. It was broad daylight, the sunlight in the room bright enough to hurt his eyes. Jacob blurted out:

"How is she?"

"She'll be all right," Sean said with complete assurance.

"Thank God for that." Jacob dropped back on to his pillows, a wave of exhaustion sweeping over him. He closed his eyes against the sun and as he did so Dulcie came in, carrying a tray which she placed on the dressing-table, then pulled down the blind at the sun-filled window. She wore a navy-blue housecoat, with a wide white belt encircling a waist as slim as a girl's. She brought the tray across and placed it carefully on the bedside table, moving the telephone, the alarm clock and a notepad.

"Good morning, sir."

"Good morning, Dulcie."

She looked tired but determinedly bright. Her skin, so finely wrinkled and dried, had a leathery look which made the blue of her eyes vivid. She turned and went out briskly, and the door snapped to. Sean, throughout all this, sat on the arm of the big chair near the window, the reading chair. He stayed there, while Jacob hitched himself up and poured out two cups of tea. The ticking clock showed that it was half past nine. Sean had the massiveness, the ruggedness, of a bull.

Jacob sipped the hot tea, and said: "Coming for yours?"

"I like it cooler. Jacob, I didn't want to wake you so early but I had no choice. The local Press and possibly the police will be here in half an hour or so — the police will want to make sure it wasn't attempted murder — and you have to be wide awake and with your wits about you when they come."

"Do I have to see the Press?" Jacob asked, but was more troubled by thought of the police.

"If you don't they may wonder why and start probing," replied Sean. "You'd be wise to see them."

"I suppose so," Jacob conceded reluctantly.

"Jacob," Sean said, with a show of embarrassment which was rare in him, "I think you have a lot of problems. I don't want to make them worse than they are but I'm sure you need to understand them in order to face them."

"Which problems in particular?" The tea was still stinging hot.

Sean's gaze, beneath his thick eyebrows, was very straight.

"*Are* you going to leave Anne?" he asked, very deliberately.

As deliberately Jacob replied: "Yes."

"Why?"

"Do you need to ask?"

"You've not been particularly happy," Sean said. "But you've held on to the marriage for a long time. Are you sure you want to break it now?"

"Yes," Jacob said. "I am quite sure."

"Because of what happened last night?"

"Oh, no. I've wanted to for many years," Jacob replied.

"Even though the thought of losing you made Anne want to kill first you and then herself?" asked Sean, in a flat voice.

Jacob drank more tea and settled back on his pillows as Sean came across and picked up his cup and began to drink. Standing like that he was an almost menacing figure. His eyes were over-bright; he could not have had much sleep but that could hardly explain his forbidding, disapproving manner.

"Sean," Jacob said, "I'm not going on with this interview, I've lived with Anne far longer than I should. I've made myself go on because of what she might do to herself, how she might be hurt, how the children might be hurt. I can't go on any longer." When Sean made no comment he went on: "I can't be blackmailed by her or by you into trying to patch it up. I don't know what you're trying to do, Sean." After a pause, he enquired: "What *are* you trying to do?"

"Make you see the situation as it is," Sean answered promptly.

"I know exactly how it is."

"Do you?" When Jacob didn't answer, Sean went on: "Do you think your mistress will go on, in these circumstances? Knowing that by breaking the marriage you may well drive Anne to suicide?"

Jacob placed his cup down firmly, then settled back on the pillows.

"That will be for Vanessa to decide when she knows what happened last night. I can't speak for her. Whatever she decides to do, I shall not go on living with Anne, and nothing will make me. You can't speak or think for me, either, you know. You're not my conscience, Sean: I think it's time you stopped trying to be." When Sean made no comment, Jacob went on: "Didn't you realise how things were between Anne and me?"

"I thought you were reconciled to it," Sean said gruffly.

"Then I hid my feelings from you very well."

"Or else I was blind," Sean said. "Perhaps I knew you too well to see you objectively, Jacob —" he put his cup down in turn and went back to the arm of the chair, moving and speaking with obvious effort. "Do you have to leave Anne and break the marriage in order to find happiness with Vanessa?"

Jacob sat very still; much more tense.

"Go on," he said. "What alternative do you suggest?"

"Could you go on as you are?"

"Wife at home and mistress in some love nest? Is that what you mean? Or Anne here, mistress of all she surveys and meeting Vanessa in hotels, furtively, secretly. Is that what you really think I should do?" Jacob's voice was thick with anger. He was seeing Sean as he had never seen him before, and could hardly believe it was his old friend talking like this, and Sean's stiffness betrayed his own awareness of the constraint which had come between them.

"It happens, often," Sean replied. "You make it sound worse than it is."

"I make it sound exactly as it is."

"Jacob, when I told you Anne was alive you said 'Thank God for that.' Are you sure she doesn't mean much more to you than you realise? Or want to admit?"

"Yes," Jacob said. "I'm quite sure. But I don't want to be responsible for —" He broke off, abruptly, realising the significance of what he was going to add.

For the first time that morning, Sean smiled. He stood up, but did not move towards Jacob as he said quietly:

"You don't want to cause her death, is that it?"

"Would anyone want to cause another human being's death?"

"Leave her, and I think she probably will kill herself," Sean said. "Will your Vanessa kill herself if she can't marry you? Will she?" When Jacob made no comment, he went on with sudden harshness: "Face it, Jacob. If you leave Anne she will almost certainly commit suicide. You've seen absolute proof of how she will react. She might — I'm not sure but she might try to kill you again. She might even attempt to —" He broke off, as Jacob had a few moments earlier, and for a few seconds Jacob did not realise what he meant. Then it dawned on him with awful impact.

"You mean —" He almost choked. "You mean she might try to kill Vanessa?"

"It's possible," Sean said evenly. "I really believe it's possible. Jacob, there are some things I haven't told you. Anne has been terrified of losing you for years. Since the children began to leave home she has seen you as her only — only companion," he added lamely.

"You mean possession," Jacob rasped.

"All right — possession." Sean did not argue at all. "Without you she probably won't have the will to live. Jacob —"

Jacob said: "I think we've talked enough. Why were you so anxious to see me before the Press and the police?" he added with a change of tone.

"Jacob, there's nothing I would rather see than your happiness," Sean declared. "That may sound trite, but it's true. Ten years ago I thought you'd leave Anne, and if you had done so then, it might have been all right. Now, you could never be happy if you knew she had killed herself because you'd left her. And if your Vanessa is a worthwhile human being, she couldn't, either. I can't stand by and let you step out of one hell into another. Don't you see that? I just can't do it."

Jacob felt as if there was a cold hand at his heart. He understood something of what was going on in Sean's mind, the sense of distress. Worse: he could see that Sean was right, that there would always be a ghost between them if he left Anne and she did kill herself.

And, out of his knowledge of her, he believed that she might. He closed his eyes to try to shut out the vision, and asked roughly:

"What about the police? Why are they interested?"

"They know Anne was at the hospital, that she took an overdose of the tablets I gave her. They do not know whether she took them deliberately, by mistake, or was given them. If it was just an overdose because she's been sleeping badly, that's one thing. But if it were attempted suicide after attempted murder that's another."

"Who will tell them about it?" Jacob demanded aggressively.

"These things get around."

"Not through me."

"Nevertheless you might, being angry, bitter and resentful, let something out," Sean answered stubbornly. "I told Dulcie to clear the wet clothes away from the cloakroom, and she won't say a word. But pressed by questions you might have let the cat out of the bag if you hadn't been warned." After a pause, he went on unhappily: "Jacob, I would be less than a friend and less than a doctor if I didn't warn you that if you go on with this *affaire* with Vanessa, Anne will probably try again. You would never be able to keep the truth out of the newspapers if there were an inquest. These are simple fact. I wish to God they weren't."

Jacob echoed: "Simple facts, are they? I would like to know some more simple facts."

"I don't understand you," Sean said.

"And I certainly don't understand you," retorted Jacob. He flung back the bedclothes and climbed out of bed, pyjamas rucked up about his long legs. "You aren't behaving like the man I know. You've been talking as if you were someone else. The you I've known so long wouldn't wish me to go on living with Anne, you'd be much more likely to advise me to leave. What's happened to you, Sean? Who's been getting at you?" He stood in front of Sean, a head taller, glaring down in sudden anger. "Come on, let's have it. Who's been getting at you? Who's told you all the fancy things? Is it *Anne*? Has she been getting at you? Has she made a fool of you?"

Sean said stiffly: "I've told you what I believe to be the truth."

"I daresay you have. Who put you up to it?" As he raised his voice Jacob found it difficult not to grip Sean by the shoulders in an effort to shake the truth out of him. For once the possibility had occurred to him, he had felt sure that Sean was voicing someone else's ideas, rather than his own. "Come on — let's have some more simple facts!"

Sean said, wearily: "All right, Jacob." His eyes were burning. "I've been very worried about you and Anne for a long time. She's been to see me about not sleeping. She's told me she felt sure you were seeing another woman, and were planning to leave her. Until I gave her those tablets she had hardly slept for weeks. Did you know that?"

"She's always complained about not sleeping but —"

"You put it down to her restlessness, didn't you?" Sean interrupted. "Her nervousness — to missing the children and worrying about them. Well, the real reason was worry about you."

Jacob said, tautly: "So she's been talking to you pretty fully."

"She had to have a confidant."

"And she persuaded you to do everything you could to persuade me to stay with the marriage," Jacob growled. "Aren't doctors supposed to be impartial?"

Sean caught his breath.

"Doctors can be. Friends can't."

"Then you shouldn't try to judge," Jacob growled.

"You couldn't be more right," said Sean in a hard voice. "You can't be a doctor and impartial when emotional and neurotic symptoms are the rule. So, I didn't try to be." He drew a deep breath, and held his head high. "I sent Anne to see a psychiatrist."

Astonished, Jacob simply gasped: *"What?"*

"She came to me in terrible distress. She said that if she lost you she would kill herself. She said a lot of other things, too. I am a family doctor. I can help in most things but I can't help anyone who is mentally sick. That is a specialist's job. But I'm not a great believer in Freudian psychology, and I didn't want Anne lying on a couch and digging into her past. I sent her to a man I trust before anyone else in this field — to a Dr. Emmanuel Cellini. Do you know of him?" Sean finished abruptly.

Still astonished, Jacob said: "No. Why didn't you tell *me?*"

"Because Anne was my patient and she went to see Cellini on condition that I didn't tell you. I'm telling you only because of what happened last night. And what happened last night is exactly what Dr. Cellini told me to expect." Now, Sean began to pace the room. "I saw him again before coming here this morning. I've told you what he told me. His professional opinion is that Anne might kill herself, will conceivably try to kill you before letting you go to another woman, and might kill the other woman. He said —" Sean broke off, faced Jacob squarely and went on savagely: "He said the only reasonable hope for her was to keep you. That if this *affaire* of yours was a passing one, an infatuation, then Anne might recover, but she has gone so far into obsessional neurosis that it's virtually impossible to pull her out of it. If you leave, all her resistance will be gone, she will be —"

Jacob interrupted in a searing voice: "Are you telling me that he said she is mad?"

Sean caught his breath.

"*Are* you?" Jacob demanded. "Am I married to an insane woman? Is that the official psychiatric opinion? Come on, Sean, I want to *know*. Or is this just a lot of mumbo jumbo? Is this Cellini simply a quack? Come on — tell me!" Now he actually gripped Sean's shoulders with hard fingers.

Sean said, as if every word hurt him: "You must see Cellini yourself."

"My God I must! And this talk about the newspapers and the police — did the precious Dr. Cellini put you up to this, too?" He actually shook Sean, whose body rocked but who made no attempt to free himself. "What is it — a conspiracy to keep me chained, body and soul, to a woman who is liable to try to kill me any time I happen to look at another woman?"

Still painfully, Sean said: "If either the police or the newspapers find out about last night, they'll have to be told everything. If they know Anne is a patient of Dr. Cellini they'll know that she's not been well for a long time. And they'll probe. Anne *did* try to murder you, didn't she? Attempted murder *is* a crime. We can hush it up or we can have it splashed over the newspapers and Anne can be charged. What's it to be, Jacob? Are you going to keep the secret, and try to make sure Anne doesn't attack again? Or are you going to tell the world? It has to be one or the other. Don't make any mistake about that."

At last, he raised his hands, gripped Jacob's wrists, and prised his fingers away. But he did not release Jacob; he kept him there, his grip now much fiercer than Jacob's had been; and his eyes blazed with a kind of demanding anger, a demand for an answer. His manner, his grip, his blazing eyes, all told Jacob that he, Sean, believed the responsibility was wholly on him.

As they stood, as Jacob's anger rose in him to match Sean's, there was a tap at the door. Jacob heard but did not heed it, until it was repeated. Then he called in a voice tautened by his anger:

"What is it, Dulcie?"

"There's a gentleman to see you, sir," Dulcie called in her clear, frail voice. "It's a policeman, a detective."

Her own alarm showed clearly in her voice.

Chapter Nine

QUESTIONS

Dulcie's alarm and anxiety showed in her face as Jacob opened the door; there was appeal in the faded eyes, too; for once she looked her age. And she seemed so small; shrivelled up. Her appearance shocked Jacob, who drew back.

"Where is he?" he asked gently.

"I asked him to wait in your study, sir."

"Tell him I'll be down immediately," Jacob said. "Did he give his name?"

"It's Detective Sergeant Wallerby, sir."

Wallerby was the detective responsible for King's Narrows, and the whole of this western part of the Mildern Borough, now part of the London Metropolitan area. Jacob knew him well by sight, casually by acquaintance on civic committees and at the golf club, as a neighbour more than as a police officer.

"That's all right," Jacob said.

Dulcie was looking at him, near-despair in her eyes; and then she glanced at Sean, as if it was his presence that tongue-tied her. And then, clearly driven by a compulsion too strong to resist, she said:

"You won't — you won't tell him anything, sir, will you?"

Jacob could have asked: "What is there to tell?" or he could have rounded on her and asked her what she meant. But there was no time, and he must not add to her distress. He put a hand on her shoulder.

"Don't worry, Dulcie."

"I — I couldn't bear it if they said she tried to kill herself," Dulcie went on in a broken voice. "I just couldn't bear it."

"She just took too many sleeping tablets," Jacob said, still gently.

For the first time since Dulcie had come, Sean said gruffly: "Yes. Don't get any ideas into your head, Dulcie." He pushed past Jacob, saying gruffly: "I'll go and have a word with Wallerby." He gripped Dulcie's arm as he passed her, heading towards the door. Now Dulcie put out her hands as if she needed more reassurance; she looked so very frail as she whispered:

"They'd say you drove her to it, sir. I simply couldn't bear it."

For the first time, Jacob wondered what was really passing through her mind, what she felt, how she regarded him and Anne. There was such a heavy burden on her, although he had never noticed it before. Suddenly there were a dozen questions he would have liked to ask her but this wasn't the time.

"We'll talk later," he promised. "Try not to worry."

Then he turned back into his room.

He hadn't shaved, but it wasn't really late, that wouldn't look strange. Yet it was late not to be up and dressed. He pulled on a pair of slacks, an undervest and a short-sleeved shirt, socks and house shoes, and brushed his hair. He hurried downstairs, hearing voices from the study, and turned into it. The room caught the morning sun, and was very bright. Perhaps by design, Wallerby had his back to the window, so that Jacob could hardly see his face, with the craggy features, but had only awareness of a man much bigger and powerful-looking than he had remembered.

"Good morning," Jacob said, and wondered whether to say 'Mr. Wallerby' or 'Sergeant'. So he used neither, and Wallerby set the tone.

"Good morning, sir. I'm sorry that your wife had such an upset last night."

"Thank you," said Jacob. "It's most distressing, but I gather from Dr. McNamara that she will soon be fully recovered."

"So they told me at the hospital," confirmed Wallerby. "So it could have been a lot worse."

Jacob thought: he's here for a purpose I don't know about. He felt a tremor of alarm, but at the same time, felt more himself. Anne had taken an overdose of sleeping tablets because she had been sleeping badly; that was the story he would tell and there wasn't the slightest reason why the police should doubt it. So his voice was calm and his manner perfectly poised:

"Obviously it could have been much worse — she might have died."

Wallerby asked, in his pleasant voice: "Have you any reason to think that was what she intended, sir?"

* * *

Jacob heard the question with a great sense of shock, but outwardly he fought against showing it. Yet his mind began to race and his fears erupt. Would Wallerby have asked such a question without a good reason?

He said, stiffly: "No reason whatsoever, Sergeant." But his heart raced faster than ever.

* * *

Detective Sergeant Wallerby thought: He's lying. He didn't like that question at all. And he thought. Should I push now, or pretend I'm convinced. The thoughts took only a split second to pass through his mind, and the answer came almost as quickly: let him sweat. So he smiled, and went on in the calmest of voices:

"How badly has she been sleeping, sir?"

"Very badly, I believe."

"Can't you be sure, sir?"

"No. We have different rooms," Jacob explained with great precision. "I don't really see the point of these questions, Sergeant."

Wallerby's response was challenging: "Don't you really, sir?"

"No. My wife has suffered from insomnia for years. Dr. McNamara has treated her for it. Last night, obviously, she took too many tablets."

"Do you know how many, sir?"

"No."

"Don't you know how many were in the bottle?"

"No."

"Did she go to bed earlier than usual or talk about her night, sir?"

Why *was* he asking these questions, Jacob asked himself. It was more difficult now to sound calm and to answer without hesitation; but he had to, he had to make Wallerby believe last night had been like a hundred nights before it. Yet there was the man, his questions in themselves a kind of accusation; and there had been Sean's manner, and Dulcie's: it was as if everyone knew a great deal more than he.

He lied: "No."

"Did she go to bed earlier than usual or talk about her insomnia?"

"No," Jacob said. "Sergeant, what *is* in your mind?"

Wallerby pursed his lips. Though he still stood against the window Jacob had become more used to the light, and could see the other man and his expression, was aware of the very deepest, very bright eyes, the big jaw, the almost trap-like mouth.

"Well, sir, this particular drug — Pentomine — is a particularly dangerous one in some circumstances. It is only prescribed in acute cases of chronic insomnia. You did not, by any chance, give them to her, mistaking the dose of course?"

Jacob felt a sweep of emotions running through him. Anger; fear; exasperation, indignation; concern — and anger again. What right had this man to talk to him in such a way? And why did Sean stand there saying nothing; it was almost as if he, Sean, had prompted these questions, not simply anticipated them.

He said stiffly: "No I did not."

There was utter silence in the room, and it seemed to be an accusing silence.

In the midst of it, Jacob thought: but I've done nothing to be accused of. Wallerby's trying to frighten me, but I've nothing to fear from the police. And his thoughts ranged now at furious speed, over the years to the first half-truths he had told to Anne, so laying the foundation to their unhappiness, leading directly to this moment. Sean wanted him to keep silent; Dulcie wanted that, also. But why? Simply because, as Dulcie had said, he would be thought to have driven her to try to kill herself.

Good God!

He was on the point of accepting responsibility, guilt, blame for something *he* had never done. *He* hadn't given her those tablets, or urged her to. That had been her responsibility. And she, Anne, had struck him and pushed him into the pool, *he* hadn't pushed her. What was this conspiracy to make him conceal the truth?

Thinking with a kind of desperation, he was taken by surprise when the telephone bell rang. He started. Wallerby did not even glance towards the instrument, but Sean did.

"Shall I get it?"

"No thanks." Jacob did not know whether to be glad or sorry about the interruption: at least, it gave him a little time to think. The ringing sound exaggeratedly loud. He moved and plucked up the receiver.

"Jacob Stone," he announced.

"There was a kind of gasp at the other end of the line, and then Vanessa said:

"Oh, darling, then you're all right."

* * *

She had never telephoned him here before.

He had not dreamed for one moment that it would be her, and there was not the slightest hope of hiding his surprise, almost his alarm, from the others. He was aware of them staring at him, waiting for him to speak. And he was aware of the fact that Vanessa was waiting for some word of reassurance, that as the seconds ticked by, she must be feeling puzzlement, even alarm.

"Jacob! Are you there?" she asked, and he fancied that her voice echoed about the room.

At last, he answered; and at last he decided what to do. As the decision came, he felt as if a great burden had been lifted from him, and the sense of tension and of fear departed.

"Yes, darling," he said, warmth deep in his voice. "I'm here all right. And I want to see you as soon as I possibly can. Are you —"

"Jacob! What's happened?" Vanessa asked.

"I can't tell you over the telephone, but I'm perfectly all right. Why —"

"Oh, darling," she interrupted. "I had the most awful dream last night. That's why I broke the rule, and called you. I dreamt you were in terrible danger, and there was no one to help you. Jacob, you *are* all right, aren't you?"

"Yes," he assured her, and there was a light note in his voice. "Hold on a moment." He put his hand over the mouthpiece and looked at Sean, aware of the changed expressions of the two men, apparently startled by the switch in his manner. "Is Anne coming home today?" he asked.

"I'd rather she stayed in the hospital at least until tomorrow," Sean answered.

"Thank you." Jacob put the mouthpiece to his lips again and spoke almost gaily. "Can you come here?"

"Jacob — at your *home*?"

"Yes, and break all our rules," he said. "We can talk better here, and I ought to stay at hand. Anne had an accident last night and will be away for a day or two. And I've a police officer and our doctor with me at the moment."

The pause which followed lengthened. He began to wonder whether it had been a mistake to invite her here, whether it would seem callous or inconsiderate, even embarrassing. Obviously, both Sean and Detective Sergeant Wallerby were still affected by his change of mood, while he felt fully resolved: whatever the consequences he would tell the truth.

Then Vanessa asked quietly. "When shall I come?" It was so like her not to enquire about the accident.

"Can you be here for lunch — at half past one, say?"

"Yes. I'd like that very much. But Jacob, are you sure this is right? I mean from your point of view."

"I'm quite sure," he said. "Quite sure." And then he realised that he wasn't justified in simply saying 'accident'. It was another of the half-truths he told too often. So he explained quietly: "She took an overdose of sleeping tablets."

"I'll be there," Vanessa promised. "Goodbye, darling." She would never know what that quiet acceptance of the statement meant to him; how much it strengthened him.

He turned to face the two men. They had had plenty of time to recover, and Wallerby was quite expressionless, even though from where he stood Jacob saw him in the full window light. Sean looked baffled — and very, very tired. Each man waited for him to speak.

He smiled, completely in control of himself.

"I think I'd better fill in some gaps, Sergeant," he said. "I first thought it would be better to keep some parts of the truth secret, but I've changed my mind. The truth is, I had a quarrel with my wife last night. I asked her for a divorce, and it made her very angry and very upset. And apparently she had suspected that I was in love with another woman, and this was one of the causes of her insomnia. Perhaps the main cause. In view of this, there is an obvious possibility that she did attempt to commit suicide; in fact when I found her, I took that for granted. So you see, you were right, at least about that."

He was glad that it was said; glad to see the puzzlement in Sean's eyes, with some relief, too: at least he had not needed to say that Anne had first tried to kill him, had taken the tablets assuming he was dead.

"I'm very glad you told me," said Wallerby stiffly. He hesitated, as if not sure how to say what was in his mind: "Part of our job is to try to prevent crime, sir, to help — everyone. And we can only help if we know all the circumstances."

"Yes," Jacob said, drily. "But some things are outside your sphere of influence, aren't they? I mean: if a marriage breaks up and one partner is so distressed that he or she thinks it's not worth living, what can the police do?" When

Wallerby looked too startled to reply, Jacob went on: "If there *is* anything you can recommend I would very much like to hear it."

Wallerby ran his fingers across his chin and said in a rather rueful voice:

"There's nothing I can do officially, sir, but I will say one thing: the reason I came this morning, the reason I pressed you as I did, is that Dr. McNamara let it out that your wife consulted Dr. Emmanuel Cellini. And Manny Cellini is often a kind of last resort, sir. I suppose you could say it's none of my business, but I hope you won't. If I had your kind of problem on my hands I would consult Dr. Cellini. He certainly wouldn't do any harm and he might do a great deal of good." Wallerby paused before turning to Sean and going on very heavily: "Wouldn't you say so, doctor?"

Sean seemed to start; to draw himself up as if waking from a trance; and then he said:

"Yes. Yes, certainly."

"From what you've told me," Jacob said, "I think we should both see him. Is there any hope of his coming here this afternoon, say? About four o'clock?"

Chapter Ten

FIRST VISIT

"Jacob," Sean said at the door, "are you sure you're doing the wise thing?"

"Yes," Jacob answered firmly. "I'm going to make sure that all the cards are on the table. I've lived too long covering up, pretending, lying to myself, to Anne and to others."

"You won't forget Anne in all this, will you?"

"I won't forget anybody," Jacob said. "Not even myself."

Sean laughed; it was almost the first really natural thing he had done since he had arrived. Wallerby, easing his car forward on the drive, must have heard it; he glanced at them, raising a hand from the wheel. Dulcie, coming along the passage, must have heard it also, although she didn't pause on her way up the stairs. Sean went off, racing his Jaguar as if he meant to catch up with Wallerby; in fact, catch up with everybody on the road.

The grandfather clock began to strike... nine, ten, eleven. Jacob looked all about the sunlit grounds and was tempted to go out, but instead turned back, wondering what to say to Dulcie. He carried a mental picture of her wizened face, her frightened expression, as he went into his room. She had just finished making the bed, and had the morning tea tray in her hands.

Every question in the world seemed to be concentrated in her eyes.

"Is everything all right, Mr. Jacob?" She was pleading for reassurance.

"In some ways, yes. In others —" He broke off. "Go down and make me some toast and coffee, and I'll come and have breakfast with you in the kitchen."

Momentarily, her eyes lit up. She turned, with the tray.

"And Dulcie, we'll have a guest for lunch, and probably two guests for tea," Jacob added.

"I'll see to it," she said. "I've lamb chops for lunch."

"That will be fine. I'll be down in five minutes."

In fact, he shaved and showered, and was down in the kitchen in a little more then ten minutes. Dry toast, cool and crisp, was in a rack, coffee was still percolating. An oaken Windsor armchair, used by his father and his father before him, was drawn up at one side of an old deal-topped table, spread halfway with a linen cloth. An Aga range, not used now, stood behind him; wide windows which overlooked the vegetable garden and some sheds, faced him. In a corner was a rocking chair with leather padded arms, seat and back, and a freshly ironed antimacassar.

"Sit down, Dulcie," Jacob said, and she sat in the rocker, and folded her arms, hands in her lap. "Dulcie," he went on, fighting to maintain his new-found calm, "I suppose you've known that things weren't well between my wife and me."

She said: "For a long time, sir."

"Do you know what she did last night?" asked Jacob.

"Yes," she said. "I know."

"And you've probably guessed it's because I can't go on as I have been doing," Jacob said.

Dulcie drew in her breath and clenched her hands, her reply showing more tension than he had ever known her to display.

"It is a miracle you've gone on for so long sir. No one who knew the situation would have blamed you if you'd left ten years or more ago." When she went on her words were hardly audible. "I would never have stayed here, but for you. I've grown accustomed to Mrs. Stone. but — but she hasn't been an easy mistress to contend with, sir. If it hadn't been for you and the children I could never have stayed. And —" She paused, and then went on explosively: "But it's not my place to say these things. There's just one thing I *beg* of you, sir — whatever she does, whatever happens, don't blame yourself. You're not a young man any longer, if ever a man deserved some happiness, it's you. It would be terrible if you spoiled the chance just because you blamed yourself. It isn't your fault, sir. I beg you to believe me. *Nothing* is your fault, and it couldn't be, whatever happened now. Don't — *please* don't try to patch things up, sir."

He could hardly believe this was Dulcie speaking with such vehemence, such intense feeling. Mild-mannered, quiet-voiced Dulcie, who seemed to notice nothing, to hear nothing, simply to go about her daily chores.

"Dulcie," Jacob said, unsteadily, "I didn't realise that you'd noticed anything much was wrong."

"I'd have had to be blind and deaf not to, sir." Dulcie stood up from the rocker and came towards him, hands outstretched. He took them firmly. "I said it was not for me to talk, but I think perhaps I was wrong. I think I've been wrong not to speak my mind before. There are some women who seem to suck the life, the very *blood* out of a man, and Mrs. Stone's like that, sir. Every minute of your time, every hour of the day, she's demanded from you. It's — it's been agonising to watch."

"Dulcie —" he began, almost in anguish.

"Please let me finish," she said, talking over his interruption. "I may never be able to pluck up courage to talk like this again, Master Jacob. You haven't been able to move without her wanting to know where you've been, who you've been with. And if she ever thought you looked at a woman that woman was *never* invited here again. And you didn't realise she was so — so wickedly possessive. She didn't want you to live any kind of life of your own."

Jacob sat, looking up at the face now so alive with passion, feeling the biting grip of the old, thin fingers. He was astounded at the depth of her feeling, at how much she knew.

"I don't know whether you realise it, sir, but that's why the children went off. The girls couldn't be disloyal to their mother yet at the same time they couldn't stand by and watch you suffer. And Master Anthony was terribly upset because you sometimes quarrelled so. Until a few months ago I didn't really think there was any hope, sir. I thought Mrs. Stone had really drawn all the spirit out of you. Forgive me, but that *is* what I thought. She'd drawn the very manhood out of you, sir, until you couldn't fight back."

God, he thought: my God!

"And then you came back one evening, sir, like a man transformed. It was a night when Mrs. Stone had been out for tea and been persuaded to stay — at Dr. McNamara's, sir. So she was out when you arrived. And I saw you and I'd never seen you look as you did then. *Happy*, sir. Radiant. That's the only word." Now Dulcie held his fingers so tightly that she hurt. "I remember thinking: he's met someone. You were a different man. You looked *years* younger, you hadn't any worries — you, well, it was like a miracle, Mr. Jacob."

There were tears in her eyes and some even spilled down

her cheeks. But she did not let go of him. And he could not bring himself to speak.

"Then — then I realised that she would never let you go, sir. She was very clever, at first she pretended that she didn't realise there was anything the matter, you didn't know she was aware of it, did you?"

He found himself whispering: "No."

"She *was* very clever, sir. She began to talk much more of how lonely she was, how she missed the children, how much she loved you, how you were her very life. And every time you snatched a few hours I saw how eager you were, how happy you were. It was like escaping from a prison. But when you came back, there she was, like a leech, a *vampire*, sir!"

"Dulcie," he said, as sharply as he could. "You mustn't talk like that."

"I'm sorry," she said, with a kind of arrogance, "but I've got to have my say. If I drew back now, sir, I would never be able to live with myself. She has drawn the very blood out of you over the years. And now look what she's done. The moment she really thinks you've turned away, the first time you've shown her that you've got a life of your own and that there is someone who really cares, sir, she pretends to try to kill herself."

"Pretends! She nearly —"

"Forgive me, sir, but she didn't take enough to kill herself, you can be absolutely sure of that. She took just enough to put her to sleep for a few hours, to make you think she really would kill herself if you left her, but it was only a trick. Don't have any doubt about that. If Dr. McNamara and those people up at the hospital told the truth, you'd know she only took a heavy sleeping dose."

"Why on earth should they lie?" cried Jacob.

"Dr. Mac wouldn't give away any patient's secrets, sir.

He'd keep absolutely mum, but take it from me she wasn't anywhere near dying." Dulcie's eyes were bright and big, and she spoke as if with absolute certitude. "But Dr. Mac must know you need a rest, sir, I think that's why he kept her in the hospital." Dulcie released his hands at last and drew a few feet away from him. Her voice was husky and despite the brightness of her eyes she looked both old and tired. "I tell you I've waited for years for the day when you would break her hold, sir. Whatever you do, don't be here when she comes back. You've told her the truth now, if you're away when she comes back she'll know you mean it. If you're here she'll think that nothing's changed, that you'll always be coming up for more."

Dulcie actually raised her hands above her head as if in supplication.

"Don't go back to her," she cried. "Don't ever go back."

* * *

The words were ringing through Jacob's mind as he ate toast and marmalade, drank coffee, and watched Dulcie as she moved about the kitchen. She hadn't spoken again, nor had he said a word. Her outburst had been a greater shock, in its way, than anything that had happened. She had known what was happening for years, had simply stood by and watched, helplessly; and, if she were right, so had the children. Who else had been aware of the hidden tensions at this house? Sean? His wife, before her death? Other family friends? He realised now how few friends they had, how seldom they went out and how seldom others came here. He realised more vividly how right Dulcie was; whenever he had met an attractive woman, that woman had somehow been cut out of their circle of regular acquaintances.

But there was one thing Dulcie didn't know: that Anne

had tried to kill him. That placed everything else in a different perspective. She hadn't pretended to take a lethal dose of the tablets to impress him, because she had thought him drowned.

But she could have pretended to.

He finished his coffee, and stood up. Dulcie turned from the sink, hands wet from peeling potatoes, and now she looked old again; shrivelled. Her eyes had lost their lustre, and were damp with tears.

"I — I'm sorry, sir," she said.

"Don't be, Dulcie. You must have been storing that up for a long time."

"I have indeed, sir."

"I'm glad to know how much you've seen and how you feel."

"You do know there is a lot of truth in what I say, sir, don't you?"

"Yes," Jacob replied, for evasion would be useless. "I know, Dulcie —" He paused.

"Yes, sir?"

"I hope you'll make a special effort with those lamb cutlets," he said with an effort to be jocular. "We have a *very* special guest for lunch."

"Have we, sir?" At first, Dulcie did not understand, but suddenly she saw the twinkle in Jacob's eyes and comprehension dawned. Fast upon it came another change in her, a shift to excitement, to eagerness, and she cried: "Why, that's wonderful, sir! Wonderful." Now she looked up at him, her eyes very bright again. "Now I really *am* beginning to hope," she declared, then glanced at a mantelpiece clock, and cried: "It's half past twelve already, I'll never have lunch by half past one!"

When she had gone, Jacob was taken by a strange mood, to go everywhere in the house, even upstairs to what was known as the turret room. This was approached off the main landing by a flight of narrow stairs, at the end of which was another, smaller landing. The room, in fact a small tower, jutted out from the main house and the roof was higher. There was a gallery all round and the walls were lined with books.

On one side of the main room was a display of small arms, pistols, automatics, palm guns, Derringers, a collection his father had made. A number of Victorian lamps, the originals which had once lighted the whole house, stood ready primed for use at times of electricity cuts and failures, on two of the shelves.

At one time Anthony had practised using some of the firearms but had stopped because Anne had made such a fuss; it was as if she could not live with anyone without trying to dominate them.

Trying! he thought bitterly.

From the windows could be seen a magnificent view, spoiled to some degree by the new buildings. The large field where the hippies met seemed nearer from here.

Jacob stayed a while but soon went down. Just before half past one he stood at the window of the front room, watching the drive. He had had time to ponder and even to digest much of what Dulcie had said, and realised that he should not have been as surprised as he had. If anything really hurt it was her certainty that the house atmosphere had really driven the children away. He did not want to believe that to be the truth, yet at heart he knew it was.

Light glinted, as on the roof of a car, on the far end of the drive. Could this be Vanessa? Yes — there was her cream-coloured M.G., winding its way slowly along the drive. His heart raced as he went on to the porch; by the time he reached it the car was on the carriageway, and there was Vanessa looking for him. Somehow, he restrained himself from running to her. She waved, her face suddenly radiant.

The glimpse he caught was of sheer loveliness. She pulled up a few yards away from him, and he went forward to open the car door, then stopped, because he wanted the joy of watching her get out.

She pushed the door open.

Her long, slender legs appeared; surely no woman could swing her legs as gracefully as Vanessa from the cramped space of a small car's driving seat?

She wore a pale brown linen suit, flecked with white. Her hair was tumbling free, golden, loose, lovely. He had never seen her look more beautiful, more glowing: and he had never experienced such absolute joy as he watched her. She seemed to sense what was in him, and first she stood up, very straight, very tall. Slowly she moved towards him, her arms outstretched, and he took her hands, drawing her close in an embrace so fierce he wondered for a moment whether he had hurt her.

But no; her eyes still glowed, her face was still radiant.

"Oh, darling!" she gasped.

"Oh, my love."

"I can hardly believe I'm here."

"Nor can I." He knew there must be so many questions in her mind, no matter how she looked, and he could not leave her in ignorance for long. "Darling," he said, "you look — almost too beautiful."

"You may not believe it," Vanessa said, "but you look quite unbelievably handsome."

"I don't believe it," he retorted promptly. He was holding her at arm's length, now, scanning her face, the lines which were so fine-spun at her eyes, the smoothness of her forehead and of her cheeks. "Darling, I forced the issue last night. I'll tell you about it over lunch. I simply had to see you, tell you everything, be helped and guided by you. And I wanted so desperately to see you here. I think this is the only place where I can talk absolutely freely, where I can show you the situation as it really is."

"Jacob," Vanessa said quietly, intentness replacing the radiance, "that's exactly what I need to know: the situation as it really is. No dreams, no half-truths, no promises for tomorrow. You will be absolutely frank with me, darling, won't you?"

"As frank as it's humanly possible to be," he promised, and turned towards the house.

Chapter Eleven

DR. EMMANUEL CELLINI

Jacob talked almost unceasingly during lunch; lamb cutlets, fragrant peas, new potatoes, apple pie and cream fresh from a near-by farm, as appetising a meal as Dulcie had cooked for a long time. He talked on as they sat in the study, drinking coffee. He talked as they walked about the grounds. Now and again Vanessa asked a question, to get some point clear, but otherwise she listened, only occasionally having to prompt him.

At last, they reached the pool.

Near the spot where he had been standing where Anne had struck him, was a fallen branch. He had little doubt that she had used that. He turned away from it distastefully, letting his glance seek comfort and refreshment in Vanessa's glowing skin, her clear eyes, and mouth so full and generous. The sun was warm on them and brought golden light to her hair. He took her hands and gripped very tightly. "Darling — do you want to go on?"

She looked puzzled. "With what?"

"This," he answered. "Me. The whole sordid mess."

She put her head on one side and asked with great deliberation: "Do *you* want to go on?"

He could not stop from blurting out: "My God, I do!"

"What on earth makes you think that I might not?"

He hesitated. The truth was at hand and yet so hard to say. Her eyes, the set of her lips, seemed to demand it, but — an evasive reply would be so easy. But would it satisfy her?

Or him?

He said: "I was afraid that you might think you were partly responsible if she did kill herself."

Even saying that hurt; almost suggested that *he* thought she was.

"What nonsense!" she exclaimed. "Obviously if your wife did kill herself, it would be because of a long accumulated emotional attitude of mind, it would not be because you had met me. But darling — from what you've said she is capable of trying to frighten you into staying with her. Obviously, Dulcie thinks so too. Do you?" There was a sharp note in the last two words. "That's the key question."

"Yes," he answered.

"Jacob."

"Yes?"

"Tell me one thing, please." After a pause, and when he had nodded, she astounded him by asking: "Do you still love her?"

"Love *Anne*?" he exclaimed, in a tone not far from horror. "Good God, what put such a thought into your head?"

"It's the only possibility which really worries me," Vanessa answered, "and it's been in my mind for a long time. Darling, let me go on." She stopped him from pouring out out reassurances. "And make yourself answer, *please*. Does she matter to you? When you knew or feared that she might die, did you feel any fear? Alarm? Pain?"

Now Vanessa's grip was tight on Jacob's fingers; he had never known her eyes more demanding and searching. And he understood why this was of such vital importance to her and formed his words with great care.

"No, Vanessa. All I felt was alarm in case it would worry you, make you change your mind."

"Darling," Vanessa replied, in a rather helpless voice. "You can't change love as suddenly as that. If I thought you and Anne had a chance to live happily together, if I thought you had turned to me because I'm younger, or more attractive, or different, I don't think I could go on. I would still love you but I couldn't ask or expect you to break your marriage for me. But your marriage was in all but convention broken years ago, wasn't it?"

"Many years ago," he answered.

"Then there is only one thing which could make me turn away from you," said Vanessa, in a way which convinced him that she meant it, and at the same time filled him with new apprehension: there *was* a possibility that she would break away.

"What?" he asked, dry-voiced.

"If you told me that you didn't love me, and didn't want to go on," she answered.

"My God!" This time there was no deliberation in his response, just the two words touched as if with anguish. Quite suddenly he took her in his arms and crushed her to him, kissing her lips so hard that they must surely be bruised. It left her and himself quite breathless. But breathless or not it was not enough, and he took her in his arms again and in those moments all he could think of was carrying her off — into the house, even into the little changing shed. And the fire of desire in her eyes matched his.

He said hoarsely: "I suppose we mustn't. Until later."

"No," she said, and added with an obvious effort: "What time is Dr. Cellini coming?"

"About four o'clock."

"It must be that now!" she exclaimed in swift alarm, and they turned suddenly towards the house. Vanessa tidied her hair with her fingers while Jacob straightened his and pulled down his jacket. Then they turned towards the drive, and were startled enough to stand stockstill for a long moment.

In front of the house was an old, black, very shiny car; an early Morris, with running board and brass headlamps and brass fittings; a vintage model. At the wheel sat an elderly man, and through the big windscreen his pink face was clearly visible. He had a flowing, white moustache and white hair.

"He must have seen us," Vanessa said huskily.

"Then we've already told him how we feel," rejoined Jacob. He held her hand tightly as they went towards the car.

* * *

Dr. Emmanuel Cellini in fact, had seen them when they had been in each other's arms, and from that moment he had warmed towards them. For in spite of the fact that his profession brought him in contact with crimes and criminals as well as with much psychopathic illness and evil itself — genetic, born-in evil, in which he believed absolutely after a lifetime studying human-kind — he was a romantic. There was nothing, to him, so vicious and ugly as hate and envy and greed and jealousy in all its forms: and there was nothing so serene or sublime as love between a man and a woman.

And these two were in love. No one who was not could possibly behave with such abandon and with such complete obliviousness of the presence of others, of the possibility of being seen. Obviously sight of him shocked them and hastily they straightened their hair and clothes; then, they held hands and came towards him, not guilty not shamefaced; not brazen or overbold, either: just naturally. As they walked, he remarked what a pleasant-looking couple they were; and how lovely and attractive the woman. And with that realisation there came a flash of recollection: of Anne, this man's wife. She was at least as beautiful, and some would say she was more beautiful, but the expression of discontent spoiled her.

He had never greatly liked her, but his task was not to like, or to judge, only to seek the truth in human relationships; and, within the confines of that truth, to help.

He climbed down from the car, surprisingly nimble for a man of his age: which, although few realised it, was sixty-seven. He smiled, and he saw how quickly they responded, how they quickened their pace, as if they were eager to see him as he was to see them. As they drew closer, he was more conscious of the young woman's flawless complexion, and of the sun-tanned face and the physical hardiness of the man. Together and apart they looked not only a picture of health but of wholesomeness.

"Dr. Cellini?" Jacob asked.

"Yes, Mr. Stone."

"It's good of you to come. You did know that Miss Belhampton would be here, didn't you?"

"Yes, indeed. And I am happy that she is. How lovely this house and the grounds are."

"Thank you," Jacob said.

There seemed much more in his words than that. "I love it here," he seemed to say. And: "It's quite beautiful." And: "It's mine." Yet Dr. McNamara had told him, Cellini, that Stone was prepared to give up this house, his family home, for the sake of his freedom and this young woman — Belhampton. Could she be Sir David Belhampton's daughter? He dismissed the 'possibility' as unlikely, and went on:

"You are both aware that Mrs. Stone is a patient of mine, aren't you?"

Jacob said: "Yes."

"And so you must also be aware that her interests must be my concern," Cellini went on. He had a very slight accent, and a precision of phrasing which betrayed his mid-European origin.

"Yes," said Jacob again. He seemed a little puzzled. Perhaps the fact that he, Cellini, was his wife's doctor and would not normally be here to see them, had only just occurred to him.

"Dr. Cellini," said Vanessa Belhampton, speaking for the first time. "Why did you agree to see Jacob and me?"

Cellini smiled quizzically, and pursed his lips, actually twisted the ends of his silvery moustache. Yet he did not reply immediately. Warmed by the sun, he felt physically at his best, and was absorbing what he could of the couple, trying not to allow their appearance to prejudice him in their favour.

At last, he said: "I am your wife's psychiatrist, Mr. Stone. I have her interests at heart. I may be able to serve them best by talking to you, so that I can see things from both points of view. However" — he smiled at Vanessa — "I find it at least as surprising that you were agreeable to being present, Miss Belhampton. You do realise that I may have to ask many penetrating questions, don't you?"

"I do," she stated.

"May I — before we go in," he added, as Jacob made a

move towards the door, "may I ask if you have told Miss Belhampton what happened last night?"

"In full," answered Jacob.

Cellini looked at the reddened bruise on his temple.

"About the blow you allege your wife struck?"

"Also the fact that she appears to have taken an overdose of sleeping tablets," Vanessa put in, quietly.

That was the moment when Emmanuel Cellini knew that she had to be reckoned with, not only as a woman and this man's mistress, but as a human being with a sharp mind. "... appears to have taken an overdose..." meant that she was not only very alert, but fighting. She would fight for herself, of course, for her own future — but he had a feeling that she was fighting as much for the sake of the man she loved as for herself. He had a mental flashback to his last attendance on Anne Stone, and the way in which she had fought for her husband.

He, Emmanuel Cellini, had to admit to himself that it had never crossed his mind that this man's wife was concerned with anyone but herself. Outwardly unperturbed, he was troubled by the strength of his own feelings and assailed by sudden doubts as to the wisdom and the rightness of being here. Of course it was true that by seeing Jacob Stone he might be better equipped for advising and guiding Anne. But there was a faint sense of unease in him as he followed his host to the porch.

The front door of the house was wide open. Cellini stepped into an atmosphere of comfort and prosperity.

A door on the right was open.

"Let's talk in here," Jacob said.

It was a man's room, the emphasis on comfort rather than elegance.

Jacob pointed to a big, well-padded armchair.

"Won't you sit down, sir? And how about some tea?"

"I would like that very much," said Cellini; but that sense of disquiet, of wondering whether he had done the right thing, still lurked within him.

* * *

When she first caught sight of Cellini, Vanessa was startled on two counts. He looked older than she had expected, and yet there was an air of youthfulness in the pink cheeks, the cherubic brightness of his blue-grey eyes. He looked as if smiling came easily, while still retaining a sadness that might be of disillusion.

In addition to this, Cellini in stature and in colouring was remarkably like her own father; so was his expression. Perhaps it was one which came with age and long-suffering and years of acquiring wisdom. Jacob leaving the room for a moment to confer with Dulcie, Vanessa turned impulsively towards the psychiatrist.

"Dr. Cellini," she said. "I have one favour to ask you."

"Tell me what it is," said Cellini, non-committally.

"Whatever you think of me, please put Jacob's interests first. Don't soften any questions or keep silent about any subject because of me. Jacob is already a little afraid that, not wanting to get myself or my family involved in what could become a scandal, perhaps even a tragedy, I might be influenced against him by what happened last night. I would much prefer to face with him squarely and without subterfuge the whole matter."

She had not intended to say so much, but even as it was, she felt that she had broken off too abruptly, partly because she was disconcerted by the direct gaze from Cellini's eyes. When she had finished he nodded slightly, and then said:

"Would you keep your hold on Jacob, would you in fact afterwards marry him, if the fear of losing him drove his wife to kill herself?"

"Jacob asked me virtually the same question," replied Vanessa. "Yes, Dr. Cellini, I would. I am deeply concerned with Jacob's life. I am not at all concerned with his wife's, except as a human being. In any case I would do all I could to prevent her from killing herself, because if she did such a thing Jacob would almost certainly be haunted by guilt." She paused, then went on slowly: "Do you think she really intended to kill herself last night? You know her enough to have an opinion about that, surely."

Chapter Twelve

THREE PLUS ONE...

Yes, thought Emmanuel Cellini, I know her well enough to have an opinion. But it certainly is not a cut and dried one. I am not at all sure that she meant to commit suicide. She might have taken too many tablets because she was desperate for sleep. Or she might have been horrified at what she had done to her husband, believing him dead. Or she might possibly have intended to win sympathy for herself, from the McNamaras or from a host of friends. But I cannot tell this woman what I think about Anne Stone.

Before there was time to answer, Jacob came back.

"Tea won't be long," he promised, sinking into a chair. "Well, Dr. Cellini, I am fully prepared to answer any question you care to ask." He placed his hands on the arms of the chair, and waited.

Cellini was aware of the intense gaze of Vanessa Belhampton; of the outwardly calm manner of the man. He had an impression that Stone had come to a decision which was for him momentous, and that in consequence he had been freed from a considerable strain.

He asked: "In the twenty-five years of your marriage, Mr. Stone, have you ever wanted to leave your wife before?"

"Frequently," Jacob answered.

"For another woman?"

Jacob smiled. "No," he admitted. "This is the first time I've ever felt that I could face a second marriage. In the past, all I ever wanted was to get free."

"Why?" inquired Cellini.

The smile faded from Jacob's face as he answered: "Because I've had black moods of depression so deep that all I could think about was getting out of that marriage, of running away. It was intolerable — absolutely intolerable. Sometimes I felt I would crack under the strain."

"Why did you stay in the marriage, in such circumstances?"

"For the children," Jacob answered.

"Was that really the only reason?"

Jacob frowned in thought and retrospection.

"It isn't easy to compute reasons over twenty-five years. I am quite sure I would have left her had it not been for the children. But this house was a powerful reason, too. I knew I would have to leave her in possession, and that was a hateful thought."

"Is that the family?" asked Cellini, looking at a photograph on the mantelpiece.

Jacob nodded.

"And they were brought up, I understand, in a household ruled by hate." The bluntness of the words was eased, a little, by Cellini's soft voice.

"Hate?" repeated Vanessa.

"Yes," said Cellini. "The slow-burning hatred which grows between people who live together and yet long secretly for the strength to walk out of the marriage to a dreamed-of happiness. Tell me what kind of a life you led, Jacob. I have heard your wife's version; now tell me yours."

Hesitatingly, Jacob began to answer. Now and again he was acutely conscious that there was much he had not told

Vanessa, but gradually he forgot that and became more fluent. Yet something of past hurt sounded clearly in his voice, and when he told of their son; in infancy, childhood and then in adolescence, the pain seemed naked, and for the first time Vanessa spoke.

"So she used the boy to hurt you."

"Yes," Cellini said, to save Jacob the need, "but only out of her own hurt, surely. She may be wrong; but she will believe herself right. And so it is with Jacob."

"But to say he drove Anthony away!" cried Vanessa.

"In a way both of them did that," said Cellini. "The error is in trying to apportion the blame. Where hurt is concerned, the cause matters little. It is the hurt that counts."

"At least you can try to make sure the cause is found," Vanessa reasoned.

"Yes, indeed," agreed Cellini. "And that is precisely what I am trying to do. Find the cause of the wounding, so as to remove it. The removing may well hurt more than the wounding ever has." He turned towards Jacob and asked in a sharper voice: "In spite of all this you would be prepared to let your wife stay in your home, now."

Jacob smiled for the first time since he had told his story, looking across at Vanessa.

"Yes," he said. "It doesn't seem important any longer. What *is* important is being with Vanessa. Do you doubt that, Dr. Cellini?"

"Not for one moment," Cellini assured him. "I set great store by love between two people. Have you ever before felt that you could walk out, leaving the house and everything behind?"

"At moments of great strain, yes," Jacob answered.

"Can you tell me what incidents created such strain?" asked Cellini.

Jacob gripped the arms of the chair, and glanced at Vanessa but looked back at Cellini quickly, although he did not answer for what seemed a very long time. Vanessa stirred, brushing her hair back from her forehead; she showed signs of increasing tension. Should she be here? wondered Cellini. Had it been a mistake to see them both? His own unease returned, worsened by disquiet because of the stresses inevitable within these two people.

Suddenly, Vanessa spoke.

"Would you like me to go, Jacob?"

"I certainly would not. There is nothing I can tell Dr. Cellini that I haven't already told you. The difficulty is to explain in a few sentences. I've been groping for the right ones. Dr. Cellini, I have found most of my married life a great strain. I knew soon after the marriage that it had been a mistake but at first I thought I would get used to it, and I suppose in a way I did. I insulated myself against it in a way, so that it did not hurt all the time, and sometimes, especially with the children or with friends, it was not only bearable, it was enjoyable. Such enjoyment, however, was very soon dissolved by Anne's jealousy. Quite early in our marriage she would go into hysterics because I'd greeted an old family friend with a kiss. If I danced and she thought I was holding my partner too tightly or too closely, if I was walking in the High Street with another woman, even though a mutual friend, Anne seemed to have the fixed idea that any physical contact with another woman indicated that I wanted to take her to bed."

"And did it?" Cellini interrupted, mildly.

"No."

"You mean you *never* wanted to take another woman to bed?"

"I don't mean anything of the sort," answered Jacob easily. "I mean it had never been an obsession. Partly because of the uproar it would have caused had Anne found out, partly because I've always hated anything furtive." He paused, and then went on: "This obsessive jealousy of Anne's used to nauseate me. And it wasn't simply with other women either. I have known her to throw a fit, figuratively speaking, if she thought I was favouring one of my children. I once" — he closed his eyes — "I once went into a bathroom while Joan was having a shower; she had forgotten to lock the door." Jacob fell silent, and his jaw seemed to work as if he was gritting his teeth to keep back words. Slowly, he went on: "I was accused, in front of the child, of incestuous intent. Anne kept this up all evening and most of the night. I don't — I really don't know how I kept my hands off her."

He fell silent again; and in the silence the breathing of all three people in the room seemed to sound very loud.

"Did you ever strike your wife?"

Jacob ground out: "No."

"Were you often tempted to?"

"My God, yes!"

"Did she ever strike you?"

"Yes."

"And yet you did not strike back?"

"No."

"Are you such a saint?" asked Cellini. "Or a coward?"

Vanessa drew a sharp breath and looked angrily at Cellini, who did not appear to notice her. Veins were standing out on Jacob's forehead and in his neck.

"Is it being less than a man to try to hold a family together? Is it being less than a man to resist placing your hands round a woman's neck and choking the life out of her? I tell you —" His whole face worked, his body was at a peak of quivering tension. "I tell you that if I'd once touched her on those occasions I would have murdered her."

He stopped again, his breathing harsh and laboured.

"*Did* you ever try to kill her?" persisted Cellini, his voice little above a whisper.

Jacob's hands bunched on the desk. There was an actual rattle of sound as they shook uncontrollably. He tried to speak but the words would not come. Vanessa leaned forward and Cellini seeing this, noticing her tension, wondered whether she feared some revelation which would be new to her. As they sat, as they waited, a house martin flew close to the window, swerved, struck the window with a sharp sound, and flew off. Even Cellini started, and Vanessa jumped up from her chair.

Then Jacob said distinctly: "Yes. Once."

The sound of the words hovered; seemed to echo. Cellini, not truly shocked and yet astonished by the admission, saw Vanessa sit back in her chair. He knew that she had been aware of this; he thought she seemed glad that Jacob had told the truth. And then came a welcome break in the tension, a sound from the passage: Dulcie arrived, wheeling a tea trolley. Obviously to make sure that she could not see his face, Jacob got up and went to the window and stared out. Vanessa moved to help Dulcie with the trolley which, when in position, opened out to table size. The centrepiece was a rich fruit cake; there were strawberries and cream, wafer-thin bread and butter, what looked like homemade apricot jam. Dulcie shot Jacob a single glance but it did not linger. Cellini said clearly:

"How very appetising it looks."

Dulcie went out and closed the door, and Jacob turned round and rasped:

"I've heard her call the girls whores. I've known her got into a paroxysm of rage because our son was out late — very late — one night after playing cricket and going on to a dance. I've known her shout and scream at the children for trivial little things that should have been laughed at, and —" He was almost choking, and now his hands were bunched in front of him and he stared as if unseeing at some kind of horror. "I've known her be all sweetness and light, joking with the family, and then suddenly, when some word or action has displeased her or there has been an imagined slight or insult, she has turned into a fury, into a shrew. It was never possible to be sure what her mood would be. She might open this door and come in like a dove, or ranting like a fish-wife. And one day, in this very room, I found every drawer opened, letters strewn everywhere, all my files emptied and on the floor a report I was making for the Fine Arts Committee torn up in a hundred pieces. She thought I was having an *affaire* with an actress at the local theatre and was looking for love letters. The children were still at home. I swear that if they hadn't been I would have left her for good. But I couldn't leave them, had I done so there would have been no one else on whom to vent her rages, and they would have suffered.

"That night — I tried to kill her."

* * *

Vanessa said, in an anguished voice: "Oh, my darling." Cellini noticed her, but all his attention was concentrated on this man, who spoke as if each word was drawn out in pain. He did not think in all his life he had seen a man in such torment; had heard a more vivid story of a man who had lived in hell.

* * *

"She was nearly hysterical," Jacob went on evenly, "and there was nothing I could do to quieten her. I'd sent the children — they weren't so young, Angela was already twenty-one — into the town to see a film. As luck would have it, it was in the summer, and Anthony was home. I couldn't bear it when they saw her in these rages, and I'd never seen her in one as bad as this. She wouldn't listen to me. If I went near her she kicked and struck me. I can't begin to tell you the things she said and threatened to do. And then suddenly her mood changed and she became all contrite, and swore she wouldn't behave like it again. There had been a time when I had believed her promises but I soon discovered that such promises never to lose her temper again were simply to disarm me —" He broke off, sweating. "She would change moods and cling to me and swear everlasting love and plead with me to take her to bed, and then suddenly revert to violence, threatening to kill me if I so much as touched her."

He paused.

"She's been better lately, in a way. And there were always times, sometimes days and occasionally a week or more on end, when she was calm and reasonable and quite pleasant and liveable-with. But the slightest thing could make her switch to fury. It was like living on a knife-edge. It was hell."

He stopped again.

He was trembling all over.

He turned and put his arm about Vanessa's waist.

"It wasn't until I met Vanessa that I began to live without fear. Without dread. Vanessa somehow gave me strength. I wasn't so vulnerable any more."

Vanessa, standing still, was crying silently.

Jacob's arm seemed to tighten about her waist.

Cellini felt as if he had been through a period of intense strain, and could not bring himself to move. But at last he said huskily:

"You say you tried to kill her."

"Oh, yes," agreed Jacob.

"On the night when she searched your room?"
"Yes."
"What did you do?"
"I tried to give her an overdose in an injection of morphine."
"Did you *have* some here?"
"Yes. I had kidney stones once, and the pain was unbearable. Sean — Dr. McNamara — gave me a supply in case I had another attack. I hadn't had to use it. Anne was in a state of nervous prostration, she often was after one of her outbursts. I put in a grain, which I knew would kill her."

Vanessa's eyes were closed, but his were wide open.
"Well?" demanded Cellini.
"I couldn't do it."

His voice faded. He breathed heavily through his nostrils, and was sweating at the forehead and upper lip because of the effort of reliving a night of horror. He dabbed at his forehead, after a while, and after a long pause Cellini asked quietly:

"How did you feel afterwards, Jacob?"
"I don't quite understand."
"Sorry that you'd failed, or relieved?"
"Both, I suppose," Jacob answered with a little bark of a laugh. "Does it matter?"
"What matters is whether you would try again — if she persisted in her refusal to divorce you," Cellini said. "Would you?"

Very quietly, Jacob answered: "No."

Vanessa turned suddenly on Cellini.

"Are you really sure you're right about what really matters?" she asked sharply. "Are you sure the real question isn't whether *she* will try to kill *him* again?" When Cellini did not answer at once, she went on: "Have you really come to hush that up, Dr. Cellini? Have you come to frighten Jacob into saying nothing? Are you one of those people who believe in the sanctity of marriage vows and not in the sanctity of human beings? Did you agree to see me in the hope of persuading me to give Jacob up, to leave him? Because if you did, you have wasted your time. I told Jacob this morning that only one thing can make me turn away from him: and that is if he has a change of heart.

Cellini felt his own heart warming to her, but he did not reassure her with words, only with a smile. Then in his gentlest voice he went on:

"There is one other thing I need to know, Jacob. Exactly what you saw last night, when you were attacked."

Slowly, Jacob told him; the pale hand, the stick, the white scarf and Anne's shrouded face. He drew the picture so vividly that the others did not even glance away from him.

He stopped.

At that moment, across the silence came a crash of breaking glass. A stone hurtled against the tea trolley, sending cups and saucers, jam and cakes, flying in all directions. Splinters flew. And just outside the window, both fists raised, mouth wide open and face distorted, stood Anne Stone.

Chapter Thirteen

FURY

In the split second that followed there was a strange hush. And everything seemed still. Anne, glaring, her fists still raised. Vanessa, half-raising from her chair. Dr. Cellini, sitting with his hands on the arms of his chair, staring. And Jacob, half-turned, hands raised to his chest.

Something which had broken fell; there was a tinkle of sound.

Slowly, Jacob put a finger to his left cheek, and on the cheek blood appeared, a faint smear at first, then becoming a tiny crimson stream. Vanessa, seeing Jacob's movement, saw the blood.

"Jacob — you're hurt." Her voice was stiff. Mechanical.

"Hurt!" screamed Anne, as if she needed only that voice to release the fury in her. "I'll cut his throat! I — my God, and what I'll do to you, you whore!" She raised her voice and screamed and threatened, the words as ugly as the stridence in her voice. "Come out here, you promiscuous bitch, if you don't I'll come and drag you out!"

Jacob said sharply: "Stop it, Anne."

"Stop it?" she screeched. "You bring that whore into my house, *my* home, you're not satisfied with going around with a tart, you soil *my* house with her and you tell me to stop it! Why, I'll kill you both! I'll —" She suddenly bent down and snatched another brick from the ground and hurled it. Her aim was so bad that it struck the window frame and dropped outside, but more glass splintered and flew about the room.

As suddenly, Anne swung round and rushed away.

As quickly, Cellini stood up, and said: "I will go to her."

And Jacob said in a hoarse voice: "Vanessa, you'd better leave."

"I can't now," she said in the same mechanical way.

"You'll only make her worse."

"If I go, she will think she can order us to do whatever she wants."

"But she'll tear you to pieces, and —"

"Shouldn't we face her at her worst? Isn't this the time to see it through, Jacob?"

He looked ashen but for the blood, now dripping from the side of his chin to his neck and shirt.

"Van," he said. "She never stops, never gives up."

"Jacob," Vanessa replied, "there has to be a stand. I'm sorry it is now but if we retreat it will be defeat for good."

"Vanessa —"

"Darling," Vanessa said with a pleading note in her voice, "she's got such awful power over you. If you don't fight back now she will always have it. Dr. Cellini's here, he can see her for what she is."

"I hate you to go through this," Jacob said, hoarsely.

"I'd far rather do that than run away."

"You don't know what she can be like."

"I've a pretty good idea," Vanessa said drily, and then she put a hand on Jacob's bleeding cheek, and went on in a steely voice: "Darling, she's bled you one way or another all your married life. The bleeding hasn't always shown but it's always hurt, and it's robbed you of the strength you need to fight her. You mustn't run away again!"

In a queer, strained voice, he said: "*I'll* stay. That's not running away."

"Yes it is," insisted Vanessa. "In a funny, horrible way it is." She took a handkerchief from her pocket and dabbed the blood; and immediately the handkerchief was vivid crimson. "Jacob," she pleaded. "Please let me stay."

He gripped her arm, so painfully that she winced, then he took out his own handkerchief, rolled it into a pad and held it to his cheek. With his free arm about her shoulders, he turned towards the door. Glass crackled under his feet but he did not seem to notice. In the house there was silence, but the sound of Anne's voice was just audible, not far away.

"If she isn't stopped, she might kill *him*," Jacob said. "At least leave this to me."

He went striding towards the front door and Vanessa followed more slowly. She had a mental picture of the virago that was Anne, another of the small, delicate-looking psychiatrist; and she became as fearful for him as for herself and Jacob.

* * *

Emmanuel Cellini stared at the woman's distorted features through the broken window of the room where they were sitting. He saw a face hideous in its expression, the more so as it was a face normally judged to be beautiful. In the first few seconds he was shocked into stillness, but at last he got up, saying in an effort at reassurance:

"I will see her."

He went out.

He knew this must be a moment of truth for the couple in the room. He had time to feel a desperate sorrow for them, that their beginning should be in such tension and threat of violence, for such a scene as there had already been could scar them both, especially Vanessa Belhampton, throughout their lives. But his concern must be for the woman outside, the woman who was supposed to have been at the hospital for at least another day.

She looked quite capable of murder.

He could not hear her when he reached the front door, and stepped out, beyond the porch. Not far off, a gardener stood with a rake in one hand, cap in the other, staring at the house, no doubt staring at Anne.

Ah! There were sounds of footsteps, hurrying footsteps on stone. He quickened his pace, and as he reached the corner of the house, she appeared. She was breathing harshly, her hands clenched by her sides. There was something in her posture which thrust her bosom forward, as if she were breasting the sun and wind in a fury of defiance.

Cellini stood stock-still.

Anne stormed forward, glaring, her stance not changing. There could be no doubt that she saw him, but obviously she expected him to move to one side. He did not move at all. He was shorter than she and much more slender. Anne came on until she was no more than a yard away.

Then, Cellini smiled.

"Good afternoon, Mrs. Stone."

She seemed to snarl at him, took the remaining step forward and swung her right arm, to sweep him out of her path. Had she struck him, he would have been sent hurtling sideways. But he simply put up his right arm, took her wrist, and held it. Startled, she was taken off balance by the unexpected resistance. At once she tried to force his arm away and caught her breath with pain, although he had done no more than tighten his finger-grip. They stood together, like statues, the gardener turned to another statue, thirty or forty yards away.

Suddenly, Anne kicked at Cellini.

He could not avoid her foot without shifting his grip but he moved his leg, and the cap of her shoe caught him a glancing blow. She drew her foot back again, still snarling, and Cellini said sharply:

"If you kick me again, I shall hurt you."

"You *swine*!" she breathed, and kicked.

As she did so he pushed her arm up a little, enough to cause pain at her elbow, although he hardly seemed to move. She gave a muted scream, staggered, then went limp, giving up all attempt at violence.

"I — I'm sorry," she said, as if in sudden humility. "Please let me go."

He let her go.

She struck at him with her fist half-closed, her nails like claws. He reared backwards, and she missed. He caught her arm and twisted her round, for a moment supporting her full weight. She gasped for breath. He kept her arm high behind her in this hammerlock, and her back was towards him, all he could see was her dark, dishevelled hair and her shoulders, a blouse-shirt half off on one side.

"Let me go!" she cried.

"Not just yet," said Cellini, quietly. "I want you —"

"Let me go!"

"Soon," said Cellini.

"Ellis!" she screeched to the gardener who still stood

like a statue, "make this man let me go!"

Ellis seemed struck not only dumb but deaf, and made no move at all.

"Mrs. Stone," Cellini said, quietly, "no one is coming to your help. You must calm yourself. And I must make myself very clear. I will not permit such violence. By throwing the brick at that window you might have caused any one of three people grievous injury."

"They're lucky I didn't kill them."

"You're lucky you didn't blind them."

"I wish I had," she cried, and made an effort to free herself, only to be checked by his retaining hold. Her whole body seemed to quiver, and her breathing became sobbing, but whether of distress or fury it was not possible to judge.

"Mrs. Stone," Cellini said, "if you strike or kick me again I shall send immediately for the police and charge you with attempting to cause grievous bodily harm. Think what that would mean. Think, woman!"

He stood holding her hand up almost to her shoulder blade.

She stood within a few inches of him, straining as far as she dared without causing herself pain. She looked magnificent.

* * *

That was how Vanessa and Jacob saw her, as they rounded the corner. It so happened that the sun shone on her face, making her skin glow and her eyes blaze. And her body was angled so that she seemed to have been halted in the moment of striding forward. She looked demented; but she looked magnificently beautiful.

* * *

Jacob thought: Oh, my God.

Then he thought: And I was worried about Cellini!
Then he thought: My God, she *is* beautiful.
And next he thought: She will kill us, if she can.
And next: What will this do to Vanessa? At the thought he turned and looked at the woman by his side.

*   *   *

Vanessa stood as still as stone, half-appalled and in a curious way frightened. She saw so many things at the same time. First, how almost unbelievably beautiful Jacob's wife was. In the searching light of the sun, her skin was without blemish and her eyes seemed to radiate fire. Her closed lips were lovely in their shape and colour, and her body was quite as remarkable as her face.

She looked like Diana, caught in the moment of hurling a spear.

She had an appeal, a sexual, sensual, inescapable quality; woman incarnate. Woman, in the depths of fury because she had been scorned.

It was easy to believe that a man, taking one look at her now, would see only her beauty and would long to possess her. She, Vanessa, had thought of her in many ways but she never dreamed that she would look like this, the woman of men's dreams.

She, Vanessa, wondered with an ache in her heart: what does he think? And she made herself look at Jacob, so as to see the expression on his face.

Then, Anne glared at her.

The unmistakable venom raged out like the lash of a whip. She actually tried to move forward again, but Cellini's hold checked her. She drew in her breath with a harsh rasp, and spoke between her teeth.

"Get that woman out of here."

"Mrs. Stone —" began Cellini.

"Get her out, and — and I'll do what you say."

"Mrs. Stone," Cellini said in the gentlest of voices, "it would be better, now, if Miss Belhampton stays here. If you give me your word not to become violent I will release you, but I meant what I said. If you are violent again I shall send for the police, and charge you with attempting" — he hesitated, looking at Jacob's cheek, and went on with calm deliberation — "with causing grevious bodily harm."

Anne did not move or speak for a long time.

* * *

Vanessa thought, anguished: I ought to go.

Jacob thought, anguished: Vanessa shouldn't be here.

And he thought: I married Anne, she's my responsibility.

And Vanessa thought: But if I go, I shall have lost him.

If there was relief, it was that Dr. Cellini had said that it was better that she should stay, but for her own part she could not now understand why. It seemed that all her presence had done was deepen hideous wounds — wounds in the woman and wounds in Jacob. How could she hope to heal him now?

Jacob thought: I shall never be free of her. It doesn't matter what we do, she will haunt us all our days.

* * *

Cellini, very slowly, slackened his hold on Anne's arm. He was prepared for her to kick out or to strike again, prepared for her to launch herself at Vanessa or at Jacob; but there was at least a chance that this paroxysm had worn itself out and that at least for a while she would be calm. He himself felt very strange. The unease which had come when he had first seen Jacob and Vanessa was, in one way, much greater. For there was no doubt of his liking for them. He had a strong feeling that they were good people. Truly, simply good. And the contrast between them and this woman was almost grotesque. Yet he had been consulted about her. His professional duty was to her. And certainly she was in desperate need of help.

These things apart, he had a great problem: to decide what to do, how to treat her. Even had he not taken to Jacob and Vanessa so much, this problem would have been very grave. And he had to make a professional judgment. Was this woman truly sick, or was she what society and the Church had once deemed possessed of a devil? He did not, of course, believe in the devil. He would not, for that matter, commit himself to believing in God, but he *did* believe in Good and he did believe in Bad, whose other and more convincing name was Evil. And he did believe in genetic evil: that there were some who had evil born in them. There were times, in discussion with his friend John Hardy, Chief Detective Superintendent at New Scotland Yard, when he would agree that this evil could be bred out of human beings; that it might even have a physical cause. But he wasn't sure, for if that was how he accounted for Evil, how was it possible not to account for Good in the same way? He had a deep revulsion to thinking that Good was a matter of brain cells and metabolism. So, on balance, he came to the conclusion that Good and Evil were abstract qualities which came from where he knew not. And that in today's society, one had to accept that there was such a thing as evil incarnate; or genetic; or, if it came to that, that there was such a thing as original sin.

Was it in this woman?

Did it explain her behaviour patterns?

Or was she a self-indulged and spoiled human being so used to having her own way that whenever obstructed or denied, she ranted and screamed until she broke down all opposition — as, until a short while ago, she had virtually broken Jacob Stone's spirit?

Was she a psychopath? Irresponsible, unable to control herself?

Or did she connive and scheme to get what she wanted: not evil, as such, but basically so selfish that nothing mattered except getting her own way?

Chapter Fourteen

UNEASY PEACE

Slowly, Cellini relaxed his hold. For a moment, he thought Anne was going to fling herself at Vanessa. And, if the truth were faced, thought Cellini, any woman who found her husband's mistress in her home might be excused for flying into a rage; or being deeply hurt and resentful. To him it was absurd, to him, absolute possessiveness of man by woman or woman by man was among the most sinful offences. But he was prepared to accept this as a personal view.

He let Anne go, and she stood still.

"Anne," said Jacob, tension sounding in his voice, "Vanessa wouldn't be here if we had dreamt you would be back today."

"So doing what you do behind my back excuses you," Anne sneered.

"Anne," repeated Jacob, "last night, you nearly died."

"I'll bet you wish I had!"

Jacob caught his breath.

"I couldn't leave here and I had to talk to Vanessa," he said.

"Mr. Stone, there is no reason why your wife should not be told the truth," interrupted Cellini, nothing in his expression suggesting that he was about to lie quite shamelessly. "I wanted to see Miss Belhampton and you, and in the circumstances this appeared to be the best meeting place. The situation is quite distressing enough without you accepting more of the responsibility than is really yours. Why did you come out of hospital, Mrs. Stone? I understood from Dr. McNamara that you were not well enough to leave."

"I was well enough when I heard *she* was here!"

"How did you find that out?"

"I heard two nurses talking about it," Anne replied. "They thought I was still in a drugged sleep. Well, I was awake enough to get dressed and take a taxi and come and find her here. The moment my back is turned my husband — *my* husband, do you understand — brings this slut into my house. Why —"

And she flew at Vanessa.

Cellini was taken completely by surprise. He should not have been, but the moment she chose and the speed with which she moved deceived him. He grabbed at her blouse, but the material slid between his fingers. Vanessa was slightly closer to Anne than Jacob but Jacob moved as swiftly as she, flinging out an arm so that she ran full tilt into it. She staggered back. Jacob stepped straight in front of Vanessa, shielding her with his body. Instead of making another attack, Anne drew further back, and began to shout obscenity after obscenity, insult upon insult. "You slut, you bitch, you whore, you concubine," all these and other insults poured out and the sound and the savour of them was carried high on the quickening wind, to the ears of neighbours and of friends, to some of the hippies, to the rustling leaves and the sun-warmed air.

And as Anne raved and Vanessa stood absolutely silent, Cellini compelled himself to do nothing, so that he could see what happened next and perhaps pass judgment on it. He watched the expression on Vanessa's face change from distress to anger and from anger to despair merging to hopelessness. He watched Jacob who had known so much of this kind of raving. The others could now see his story was absolutely true, that he had not exaggerated even a little, had failed indeed to convey the savagery of his wife's venom. He saw alarm that Vanessa might be hurt change to a kind of fear, or urgency as if saying: "Go, please go," but she did not move; it was as if she had lost the strength and the will to do so.

Then a new expression spread over Jacob's face, and his manner changed with it, his body seemed not to stiffen but to relax. He began to speak.

"Anne, if you —"

She raised her voice still higher, switching her insensate fury towards him. Far off, the gardener stood and stared and there were those others, from the village, hippy camp and passers-by; watching, some appalled and all enthralled.

Slowly Jacob raised his hand and slapped his wife on her right cheek; with equal deliberation, slapped her on the other. First, this quietened, then silenced her. She backed a pace, looking at him as if she could not believe what he had done. The silence was so strange it seemed profound.

"Anne," Jacob said again, "if you carry on like that, if you swear just once more, I shall leave here. I shall sue you for divorce on grounds of cruelty. I shall accuse you of attempting to murder me. I shall spare neither you nor myself."

There was such a tone of finality in his voice that Cellini was astonished; obviously, so was his wife. She looked at him, her mouth going slack, the fire dying out of her eyes. Slowly, her body began to droop, her shoulders sagged. The malevolence which had been in her eyes faded completely, they began to mist over, as with tears. The tautness left her lips and face, her lips indeed began to pucker and her eyes to close.

She looked pitiful.

She turned slowly and made her way towards the front of the house. She did not once look back, and there was no way of being sure that her expression did not change again, but her shoulders still sagged and her steps faltered.

Cellini said, as he had before: "I will go to her."

"Dr. Cellini," Jacob said, "should Vanessa stay?"

"Of course I can't stay now," said Vanessa. "The issue is over."

The deep hopelessness in her voice could not be disguised; nor could the near despair in her eyes, in her expression. Words seemed to force themselves from her lips, each one clear and distinct, yet coming slowly as if she were giving birth to it.

She lifted her eyes to Jacob.

"Jacob," she said, "we can't go on. She is obviously a sick woman. Mentally sick. You can't walk out on her as she is now. You have to stay, whatever the cost."

Jacob said with desperation: "I can't stay with her."

"You can," insisted Vanessa. "You have in the past and you can now. You will never be free of her. You know that, really: you will never be free of her."

She turned away.

"Vanessa —" Jacob began.

"Don't, please don't plead with me," begged Vanessa, and she turned and faced him again, fire in her voice instead of the dull notes of despair. "I can't help what I've said before. I can't go on fooling myself, and nor can you. We haven't a chance together. Not a chance at all. I had thought she was just a vain and spiteful woman, even psychopathic in her jealousy, but I tell you she *is* sick, she is not responsible for her actions. You *are* the one hope she has, and you are fully aware of it." She paused, then went on: "If she ever kills herself you will blame yourself and will never stop feeling guilty. In time you will come to blame me."

"Vanessa, I swear —" Jacob began.

"You would never say so, you would never admit it to yourself," Vanessa stated with the new strength in her voice, "but you would forever blame me. It's useless, Jacob. We can't go on. She has defeated you all your life together, and she has defeated you now. She will always defeat you."

Vanessa turned, reached her car, and climbed in. The grace of her movement was as marked as ever, if a little slower. She had to take the wheel and face the two men, and for a few moments her eyes were lowered as if she could not look Jacob squarely in the eye again. She touched the ignition key and actually turned it, making a harsh grating noise, before Emmanuel Cellini spoke in that quiet but carrying voice of his.

"Vanessa," he said, "are you sure that she hasn't defeated you?"

Vanessa looked at him through half-closed eyes, and then wearily shook her head.

"I know full well that she has defeated me," she admitted. "I know I can't take Jacob away from a woman who is so dependent on him. She'll die or become a raving lunatic without him. Can't *you* see that, Dr. Cellini? Can you have any doubt at all?"

*   *   *

Cellini thought, with a despairing hopelessness: she might be right. If this is a case of over-indulgence all her life the shock of losing him could turn her mind once and for all. Whether it was that, or genetic evil, made little difference now. Either was incurable. He did not consciously think beyond that but somewhere in the back of his mind were reflections; images of what he knew to be true. If she were mad, or could be driven mad, then this man was forever her prisoner. If she were driven to kill herself, then he would be as close a prisoner as ever. Any happiness he found with Vanessa would be short-lived; there might be, there almost certainly would be, recurring spells of happiness, but the recessions, the periods of self-blame, of guilt, would get longer and get worse. Each without the other might overcome the acuteness of disappointment; might learn to live in peace. That was the best Jacob could hope for: to live in peace with himself, surrounded by a hard shell of resistance to his wife so that part of his mind rejected her. But he would be forever her prisoner, neither free nor with any hope of freedom.

But Vanessa?

It was not possible to believe that she would live alone. Somewhere there must be a man who would spark the same fires of love in her as Jacob, so that Jacob would fade into memory and she would lead a full life; the shared life. She was too lovely, wholesome, *good*, to live alone for the rest of her days.

Yet he felt convinced that if Vanessa drove off now, she would be driving out of Jacob Stone's life; while if she stayed, there might still be a chance for them.

The engine of the car started.

*　　*　　*

Jacob thought: If she goes I shall have lost her.

And he thought: But she is right, I am chained to Anne. I've stayed too long with her and the chains are too strong to be broken.

The words were like a refrain in his mind.

He could not try to persuade Vanessa to stay, he could only leave the decision to her.

He was aware of Dr. Cellini, a step or two in front of him; of distant noises; of the fact that Anne had gone back into the house, but the only face he saw, the only thought in his mind, was Vanessa.

In a voice that was hardly audible; he said: "Vanessa, don't go. At least come and talk with me."

The engine's roar seemed very loud.

"I can't stay," she replied. "She needs you."

"But last night she tried to kill me."

"Last night was last night," Vanessa said. "She was in despair. Jacob — don't make it more difficult than it has to be."

She eased off the brake and the car moved forward a few inches. One sweep round the carriageway and she would be gone in a crunching of gravel and a faint cloud of dust. It was as if the very vitals were being torn out of him.

Then, Cellini spoke. At first his voice was pitched so low that the words were hard to distinguish, but gradually they became more audible, and as they came their impact was the greater. There was not the slightest indication of the turmoil in his mind, for outwardly he was calm. And the fact that he found words difficult to utter because he was so full of doubt made those words appear to be the more positive and deliberate. It was as if the oracle was speaking.

Vanessa locked the brake, mechanically, and stared at and listened to him.

Jacob, half-turning so as to see him, seemed to hold his breath.

* * *

"Vanessa," said Cellini. "You have told Jacob that you love him. Do you truly? Is it love, to go away at the moment of his greatest need?" And when she did not answer, he went on: "If you go now, do you expect ever to come back? Or to see him again?" When she did not answer this question, either, sharpness quickened his voice. "Answer me, please. Do you expect to come back?"

"No," she said. "No."

"So this great love will be broken."

"It — it is hopeless," she said. "You must see that. It's hopeless."

"It will be, if you go."

"Don't try to make me stay!" she pleaded.

"But if you go —"

"Who are you?" she cried. "The Devil himself? You know it's wrong, you know it's cruel. To me, to Jacob, to his wife. What are you? A dealer in cruelty? Is that what you do for your patients? Torment them, torture them?" And when this time it was Cellini who did not answer, she went on: "Give me one good practical reason why I should stay. Give me one real *reason* for prolonging this agony. What good can it do to any of us?"

'A dealer in cruelty' echoed silently in Cellini's mind.

The Devil himself.

Tormenting and torturing them, until they could not bear the agony.

"Give me one single reason!" she cried. "Or else let me go, get out of the way!"

Cellini, instead of moving aside, moved towards her. Moving, he felt stronger, calmer, more sure of himself than he had since he had come here. He reached the car and placed a hand firmly on her shoulder. He was aware of Jacob, who had not moved, aware of the pain in Vanessa's eyes. Her lips were quivering, she was so near collapse.

"Do you want a reason for staying?" he asked. "Or an excuse for driving away?"

Jacob croaked: "Cellini!"

"Well, which is it you really want, Vanessa?" Cellini

asked the woman, in the gentlest of voices. "Does what you've seen here frighten you so much that you know you haven't the strength to go on with Jacob? Or are you really going because you think you will do harm here, and not good?"

"How can I do good?" she cried. "Show me a way, even a hope of a way."

"I can do that," Cellini said, with great assurance. "I can tell you that Jacob needs you. That if you go now you will leave him in hopeless despair but that if you stay you will prove how you feel about him. If you go there will be no chance for you both, if you stay there will be a chance, and even if you eventually fail you will have tried."

Her eyes seemed to burn in her face.

"They are just words," she said huskily. "Just words."

"Vanessa," Cellini said, "look at Jacob. Look into his eyes. Do you want to rob him of any chance there is?"

She stared at him for a long time.

She lifted her eyes and looked into Jacob's.

They were like that for what seemed an age before suddenly Jacob and Cellini shifted hastily to one side. Jacob's arms went about Vanessa's shoulders, her face was crushed against his chest. They did not move but their heavy breathing sounded clearly, and slowly, oh so slowly, quietened.

Cellini moved further away.

Then he became aware of two things happening, in different directions. There was movement at the front door, and for a moment he thought it was Anne; but it was Dulcie. And there was movement at the distant part of the drive: a car, coming too fast. It swung into full sight, a Jaguar which he thought he recognised — yes, there was Sean McNamara at the wheel, wild-driving, wild-looking.

"Dr Cellini," Dulcie called.

The car tore up, gravel spurting from its wheels.

McNamara flung open the door of his car and scrambled out as he cried:

"Is she all right? I'm told she came up here. *Is she all right?*"

"Dr. Cellini," Dulcie cried from the front of the porch, "she's locked herself in the turret room, and she won't answer when I call."

Chapter Fifteen

THE TURRET ROOM

Vanessa and Jacob were standing by the side of the car, Dulcie on the porch, Cellini nearest her, as McNamara strode forward. Anxiety flared in his brown eyes, he looked like a man afraid.

Cellini said: "She appears to have locked herself in what is called the turret room."

"If anything happens to her it will be my fault," McNamara growled. "I should never have let you come here. What happened? I'm told she's been in hysteria — is it true?"

"It is true," Cellini answered.

"She needs rest above everything," said McNamara, still in a growling voice. "She fooled me, she —" He broke off, and then turned to Dulcie. "Are you sure she's in the turret room?"

"Yes, sir, I saw her go in. She locked the door, and —"

"We've got to get her out," said McNamara. "Jacob! There must be another key. Come on, man, don't just stand there!"

Jacob moved away from Vanessa, looking dazed: bewildered. He was tall and lean against McNamara, who seemed now like a stamping bull. He grabbed Jacob's arm and led the way inside, as Dulcie darted out of the way.

"Dulcie," Cellini said, "we may need some hot coffee, and we'll almost certainly need Mrs. Stone's bed turned down. And when that's done will you stand by in case we need something else?"

"Very good, sir," Dulcie said. But she was looking at Vanessa, and suddenly she moved towards her, with both hands outstretched. "Please," she said, "please don't leave him. He's been so much on his own. Don't leave him now."

Vanessa said, as if some inner spirit drove the words out: "I won't, Dulcie." And they gripped hands.

Cellini's lips were moving as if in prayer of thanks.

"And don't blame yourself," begged Dulcie. "None of it's your fault, miss. It's been building up over the years."

"Thank — thank you, Dulcie."

"And don't blame *him*," Dulcie said, and she swung fiercely round on Cellini. "That policeman who was here this morning, *he* blamed Mr. Jacob. I could see he did, but it's not Mr. Jacob's fault. She — she's not normal," the old woman added, despairingly. "She just isn't normal, and his life has been hell."

There was silence.

Not far off, a dozen people watched from the fringe of the trees, and there were others among the trees. And on the road leading to Kings Narrows cars were parked, and others drew up and other sightseers came, drawn by the rumours already spreading, that poor Mrs. Stone had gone berserk. The grounds had never looked so lovely nor had the air been so balmy; and even the crowds were hushed.

"Dulcie," Cellini said gently, "will you see to the coffee and the bed?"

"Oh, yes," said Dulcie. "Yes, Doctor, I will." She gave

Vanessa's hand another squeeze and went off into the house, in the wake of the two men. Her footsteps faded.

Vanessa closed her eyes for a moment, and then brushed the back of her hand over them. At last she braced herself to look at Cellini; then away from Cellini at the ring of people.

"It will be quite a scandal," Cellini remarked.

"Yes."

"Does it worry you?"

"A scandal? Good heavens, no," Vanessa answered.

"What does worry you?"

After a moment, Vanessa said simply: "Hurting people." She caught her breath. "I hope to heaven you are right. I hope I haven't made it worse by staying." She looked at the front door, which was wide open. "I hope she doesn't kill herself."

"If she does, he'll need you even more desperately, for a while."

"For a while," she echoed bitterly, and then she raised her hands. "I'm sorry. What shall we do?"

"Go inside," he replied, and led the way.

They were near the foot of the stairs when they first heard a thudding and next McNamara's raised voice, followed by more thudding. As they started up the stairs McNamara's words came clearly from the higher stairway.

"Let me in, Anne. Unlock the door and let me in."

There was silence, before the banging started again, making it clear that she had not opened the door.

McNamara and Jacob were on the landing outside the door of the turret room. McNamara was banging on the door with a footstool. Jacob was holding a bunch of keys, and one key was in the lock. McNamara turned as the others came up.

"We've got to stop her or she will kill herself."

"What is the room like beyond the door?" asked Cellini.

"It's a big circular room, a library," answered Jacob, "with a gallery by two of the windows — it's really on two floors. She — she hasn't answered. Could — could Dulcie have made a mistake?"

"Can we get to the windows from the outside?" asked Cellini.

"With ladders, yes."

"Jacob," Cellini said, "can you fetch ladders? Is your gardener still here?" He glanced at Vanessa. "Will you go with Jacob?" It was essential for Jacob to have something to do, and in its way as vital for her. "And we may need to break the door down," Cellini added in a voice loud enough for Anne to hear.

"*Anne, let me in!*" cried McNamara.

"Doctor," Cellini said, "are you so sure she will try to kill herself again?"

"Good God, man, haven't we proof of that?"

"Indications, perhaps, but not yet proof."

"Those pills she took last night are proof enough for me. *Anne, open the door!*"

"Doctor, I think if you will rest for a while, and not shout, that might help," advised Cellini.

"Oh, do you," McNamara rasped. "Well, I don't know what's been going on here but I do know the story that's all over the village. That Jacob installed his mistress here after giving his wife enough tablets to kill herself. That she's been running wild through the grounds and that *you* stopped her with physical force. My God! To think this could have happened!"

"Doctor," Cellini said, coldly, "it would not have happened had Mrs. Stone been kept at the hospital. Why didn't you keep her there?"

"She fooled me and she fooled the nurses," McNamara answered savagely. "What a bloody fool I was!"

"In what particular way?" asked Cellini, still coldly.

"I told the nurses why she mustn't be allowed to leave," said McNamara. "I thought she was unconscious. The moment I found out —" He broke off, and went on helplessly: "The story was everywhere when at last I did learn. I came out at once, but there must be fifty cars in the road and a couple of hundred people or more. It's bound to rock King's Narrows. And if she dies — *Anne!*" he roared, and began to pound the door again.

Anne did not respond in any way at all.

* * *

Detective Sergeant Wallerby, that big and rather bovine-looking man, was very much more shrewd than many people realised. He was anxious for a step up in rank, and always looking for opportunities to bring himself to the notice of his superiors. Like all policemen in the London Metropolitan area, he had a wide general knowledge not only of his part of London surburbia but of London itself; and he knew a great deal about the senior officers whose approval he needed. He knew the consultants, too — the Home Office pathologists, the police surgeons, not only in this division but in most of the area; he knew the experts in jewels, in poisons, in ballistics, in caliographics, in psychiatry — in fact in any sphere where the police might need especial help.

Naturally, he knew Manny Cellini. In fact he had met the old man on a number of occasions, and seen him give evidence several times. Whether doing that for the police or against them, he was always the same: brilliant, lucid, immovable in his opinions. He seldom lost a case, either for the prosecution or for the defence, and throughout the police force he was both highly respected and warmly regarded. These days he seldom stirred himself, and if he did take a case then it was almost certainly because he thought that there were human factors not clearly understood.

When Wallerby realised that Dr. Cellini was involved, he was puzzled. Cellini seldom, very seldom indeed, took a straight case of a patient needing psychiatry. His interest was said to be mainly in crime.

Why, then, had McNamara consulted him over this case?

Why had he come, this afternoon, to King's Narrows?

And what was he doing up there?

Wallerby, full of these questions, had a constable in the area from two o'clock that afternoon. He was curious about the arrival of the Belhampton woman, particularly after the attempted suicide of the previous night. On the surface of it, the visit of a man's mistress to his home when the wife was in hospital, was pretty raw. When one took into account why she was in hospital, it was downright cold-blooded and callous: on the face of it, he reminded himself.

However, the influence of Manny Cellini might explain it. He was, to quote the rueful comment of police officers who had lost a case because of him, 'a Machiavellian old devil', despite his meek and mild appearance. He might well have arranged this visit to spark off a crisis, in order to learn the truth about what was going on. Wallerby was virtually certain that Cellini was the prime mover, because Dr. Mac, whatever else one said of him, was an unsubtle character, and Jacob Stone was not a man to play such a trick on his own initiative.

There was, then, a lot which Wallerby would like to know.

There was, however, one thing which he knew very well. One of the Yard's senior superintendents, a man with a great deal of influence, was Chief Detective Superintendent John Hardy, and Hardy was a close friend of Manny Cellini. There was no doubt in Wallerby's mind that he must somehow involve Hardy; the question was: how.

While he was ruminating, a flash report came in from the man at King's Narrows.

"There's something very odd going on here, sir."

"What kind of odd?"

"The woman — I mean, Mrs. Stone — is hysterical. Absolutely berserk, as far as I can see."

"You mean Mrs. Stone's up there?" Wallerby gasped.

"Yes, sir — with the other woman and Stone. There's a hell of a situation, if you ask me."

"Right!" exclaimed Wallerby. "I'll send a car down, but don't take any action unless it's obviously vital." He rang off, called the garage, found a patrol car just off duty, and then talked to the driver. "Watch what's going on up at King's Narrows," he ordered, and confirmed what he had already told the man on duty. He sent the patrol car off, and then called New Scotland Yard. He had no doubt that this was a case for direct action.

"Superintendent Hardy, please," he asked the operator.

"Just a moment," the operator said, and almost at once a man answered. "Mr. Hardy's office."

"This is Detective Sergeant Wallerby, of King's Narrows sub-divisional station," Wallerby stated. "I would like to talk to Mr. Hardy, please." He keyed himself up in case the other asked what it was about, but there was no argument, and very soon Hardy spoke in his deep, pleasing voice.

"What is it, Sergeant?"

Wallerby's heart actually began to thump.

"I hope I'm right to come to you personally, sir," he said, "but Dr. Cellini is out here, as I understand it to examine a Mrs. Stone, who allegedly attempted to commit suicide last night." He paused, but Hardy didn't speak, so he went on: "There is some kind of violence going on at the house he visited, sir, and —"

"What kind of violence?" interrupted Hardy.

"All I know at the moment, sir, is that the woman appeared to attack Dr. Cellini, and he defended himself. It —"

"Is he hurt?" Hardy nearly barked.

"Not as far as I know, sir, but he's inside the house with Dr. McNamara, a well-known local G.P." The proliferation of 'sir' underlined Wallerby's nervousness. "I don't know whether to take preventive action or not. There's been quite a scene, sir. And —" He wiped sweat off his forehead as he blurted out: "I'm pretty sure that the other woman in the case —"

"What other woman, Sergeant?" asked Hardy quietly.

Wallerby realised that he hadn't told his story very lucidly; calling Hardy had been much more of an ordeal than he expected, yet there was nothing in the Chief Superintendent's manner to imply impatience or reproof.

"I'm sorry, sir. The woman who attempted to commit suicide is the wife of a highly respected local man, sir. And apparently talk of his leaving her for another woman appears to have sparked off the trouble."

"I see. And who do you think the second woman is?" asked Hardy.

"The daughter of Sir David and Lady Belhampton, sir."

"*Who?*" Hardy really did bark this time.

"Sir David Belhampton's daughter, Vanessa, sir. She was recognised by one of the local newspapermen. I'm in charge at King's Narrows, sir, and if Chief Inspector Anderson had been at Divisional Headquarters I would have approached him. But he's been called up to the Yard, sir."

"I see," said Hardy. "Do you think there's any danger for anyone in the situation?"

"I just don't like the situation at all," Wallerby replied, still sweating. "I don't feel competent to make a decision, sir, without consulting a senior officer."

"What do you want to do?"

"Go up to the house, sir."

"Why?"

"Prevention is better than cure, sir. I've a car outside the grounds, but that's ostensibly controlling the traffic. There is bound to be a lot of scandal, and there is one of these hippy love-ins locally, quite a small one but close to the house. And in view of the people involved, sir —" Wallerby broke off, wishing to God that Hardy would say something positive. So far, he didn't sound as if he had really taken anything in.

Then Hardy said: "Go to the house alone, Sergeant. Have a walkie-talkie with you so that you can talk to your chaps. Ask to see Dr. Cellini in person, and when you see him be guided by him until I arrive."

Wallerby's heart gave a wild leap.

"You're coming in person?"

"Yes," declared Chief Detective Superintendent Hardy. "Tell Dr. Cellini so, the moment you see him."

"I'll do that, sir!" Wallerby cried, and he was so pleased with Hardy's reaction that he rang off without saying 'Goodbye'. Realisation of this omission only worried him for a few moments, however. He had an hour at most in which to work before Hardy arrived, and in that time had to show Hardy how effectively he could handle a delicate situation. He hurried down the stairs of the old police building, calling instructions to the officer on duty in the charge room. His own car, with a detective officer at the wheel, was waiting outside. He slid into the passenger seat, said: "King's House," and then sat back. A dozen people were watching, many more than were usually in this side street. He wondered if there was anyone here who didn't know about the trouble, at King's House, when the car radio squeaked, and he leaned forward and flicked the switch on.

"This is Wallerby," he said, still picturing Hardy and trying to decide whether he had handled that conversation well.

"Elliott here," a man reported. "It looks as if there is really going to be trouble at Mr. Stone's house. Mrs. Stone is threatening to burn the place down."

Chapter Sixteen

THREAT OF BURNING

Cellini watched the veins standing out on Dr. McNamara's neck, understanding and sympathising with the doctor from one point of view, puzzled from another. The only sound was of McNamara's harsh breathing. For the first time he seemed to give up. He turned slowly to Cellini and asked in a hopeless sounding voice:
"What are we to do?"
"If we gain a little time, we can surely get in from the windows," suggested Cellini.
"If she hasn't burned herself to death or thrown herself out first. She *will* kill herself. You do realise that, don't you? And if I'd kept her in hospital —"
"I shouldn't torture yourself over that," said Cellini quite sharply. "You could not stand over her all the time. Why are you so sure she will commit suicide? There were some tendencies when I saw her, but —"
"That was two days ago and it might as well have been two years," growled McNamara. "Since then Jacob has told her he wants a divorce; before then she only guessed. And his confession tipped the scales. We *must* get into that room." He turned again, as if to try to batter it down with his clenched fists, but Cellini gripped his arm with surprising strength.

"Be *quiet*!" he ordered; and as McNamara went still and silent, astounded, Cellini raised his voice still more, and called:

"Mrs. Stone."

There was no answer.

"Mrs. Stone, this is Dr. Cellini. I want to help you."

Almost at once, and from very near the door, came Anne's voice, muffled and yet with an edge of shrillness.

"No one can help me!"

"How can you tell until you've let them try?"

"There's only one man who can help me," she retorted.

McNamara caught his breath, almost ejaculated "Who?" and then felt Cellini's grip tighten and repressed the word. It was Cellini who asked in his quietest voice:

"Who is that man?"

She shouted: "Speak up! I can't hear you."

"Oh, I'm sorry," Cellini said, raising his voice. "I asked you to tell me who can help you."

"My *husband*, of course! Who else do you think?"

"I am sure he will if he can," said Cellini.

"He can all right," she called, the edge rougher in her voice. "Let him send that trollop packing and then come to me. *I'm* his wife. He belongs to me, and no one else. If you want to help me, make him send her packing."

Cellini did not respond. McNamara stared at him demandingly, but Cellini still waited, until at last the woman screamed:

"*Can you hear me?*"

"Yes, I can hear you."

"*Then why the hell don't you answer?*"

"For one reason it's such a strain speaking through this thick door," Cellini replied. "For another, I am thinking as deeply and as quickly as I can. It's no use lying to you, or promising you something I can't carry out, is it?"

"You'll never fool *me*."

"I shall never try. If you will let me come in and talk —"

"You bloody old serpent!" she cried. "If I open the door you'll all rush in and overpower me. I won't open the door."

"Then I can't help you," said Cellini, tartly.

"I tell you my husband is the only one who can do that, and his place is by my side. I'll tell you one thing, if he doesn't throw that woman out and come back to me, I'll burn the place down and kill myself in the process, and he'll have it on his conscience all his life. Make sure he knows it."

"I am sure he does," Cellini said. "Would you really take him back, Mrs. Stone?"

"I'd take him back and make sure he never got out of my sight again! He —" She broke off, and now they could hear her breathing heavily, as if she was no longer able to control herself. McNamara in turn took Cellini's arm.

"She's going into a spasm," he muttered.

"Who else is there?" cried Anne, in a wild voice. "I heard someone else. Who is it? How many are outside there? *Tell me*," she screamed, "or I'll burn the house down."

* * *

Jacob, at the head of the stairs, heard that threat; and Dulcie, coming out of Anne's bedroom, also heard it. She stood absolutely still, the colour draining from her cheeks. Jacob raised a hand to her, and whispered:

"Go down to Miss Vanessa, will you?"

"Yes, sir," Dulcie whispered in turn.

"*Are you going to tell me who's out there with you?*" Anne cried. "If you don't, I tell you I'll burn the house down under your noses."

Her voice actually quivered.

Jacob drew level with the others. He was sweating,

obviously from physical strain. He received Cellini's restraining hand calmly enough, kept his voice very low, and said:

"She's put the shutters up at the windows."

"You mean we can't get in that way?" McNamara asked, hoarsely.

"That's you, Sean — I heard you!" Anne cried. "My God what a fine doctor you've proved to be. You're no better than that psychiatrist quack you called in. I don't want a doctor, I don't want a psychiatrist, I'm not *mad*. I'm just a woman. I want my husband back, that's all the doctoring I want. Send that trollop away and send Jacob here. I'll give him all the sex *he'll* ever want. Why, the sexy bitch, if I could get my hands on her I would choke her life out."

Her voice was cracking. She sounded farther away, and perhaps she was actually moving farther into the room. There was a moment or two of silence in which Jacob drew the back of his hand across his forehead while McNamara whispered: "We can't do a thing. We haven't a chance." Then Anne cried out again, proving that she was just on the other side of the door.

"Send Jacob in to me or I'll burn the place down!"

Into the silence that followed, Jacob said in a hushed voice: "I'll have to go in."

It was never-ending, he thought wearily; tension upon tension, fear upon fear: and now he was quite sure he would have to go in to see Anne. There was a limit to resistance. He should have let Vanessa go, instead of allowing Cellini to persuade her. He vacillated from minute to minute, there was no strength in him, only changing moods of despair and hope, courage and determination and fear. There was a sound from the other side of the door, as if Anne had heard and recognised him and caught her breath.

He was preparing to call out to tell her he would come, when Cellini spoke in a clear, commanding voice:

"I must see you first, Mrs. Stone. I will then decide what to advise your husband."

"*Advise?*" she cried. "Hasn't he got a mind of his own?"

"Cellini —" Jacob began.

"He is there! I heard him, he is there! Jacob, I want to see you *now*. I'll set the house on fire if you don't come and talk to me. I mean it. I'll unlock the door and you come in alone, do you hear? If that old goat Cellini tries to get in I'll shoot him. It's got to be you and no one else. Don't you let me down!"

McNamara gasped: "Has she got a gun?"

"There is a small armoury up there," said Jacob. "That's one thing I've been afraid of. And —" He gulped. "Some oil lamps, fully primed."

"Is that a fact?" Cellini asked in a small voice.

"I use them for emergency lighting," Jacob said, and he raised his voice. "All right, Anne, I'll come."

There was a moment of utter silence before Anne cried:

"You've got to come *alone*!"

"I'll be alone," Jacob replied evenly.

"Send that old quack away, do you hear me! Send him and Sean away."

"They'll go, Anne." His face was so pale that it looked almost grey. "Both of you, please go," he said. "It's no use. You must see that now." He raised his voice: "All right, Anne." He stepped close to the door, within hand's reach. There was another period of silence, and then there came the sound of a key being turned, slowly; agonisingly.

Cellini and McNamara were now behind Jacob. McNamara stared first at his back and then across at Cellini. Neither man spoke, but very slowly, Cellini shook his head. McNamara raised his hands in a helpless gesture.

Cellini mouthed words, quite inaudible but quite unmistakable.

"She — will — kill — him — and — herself."

McNamara's eyes seemed shadowed by horror, as if he knew that this was true but felt powerless to stop it.

As the lock clicked back, Jacob stretched out his right arm to turn the handle. He felt utterly despairing but he was sure he had no choice. He had, somehow, to make his peace with Anne. He could no longer rely on help from others.

The door opened a crack.

Jacob could see the pistol in Anne's hand. She had withdrawn far enough from the door to make sure she could not be rushed. The gun seemed very steady and it was pointing at his stomach. He pushed the door wider, until both he and Cellini could see not only Anne but the room beyond.

"Tell him to go away," she ordered, and now she pointed the gun directly at Cellini. "Don't try to fool me! Make them go."

Jacob, as if startled to know they were still there, half-turned. Turning, his left arm moved towards Cellini in a gesture which said: "Go away, go away." As quietly and with as little fuss as he had taken Anne's wrist earlier, Cellini closed his fingers on Jacob's, and then tightened his grip and twisted. Jacob felt a streak of pain run up his arm to his shoulder. He was thrown off balance, and thudded into McNamara. McNamara also lost his balance, and both men staggered back, away from the door. Her face distorted, Anne squeezed the trigger of the gun. It was an obvious effort, either she hated doing it or her nerves were in such knots that she could not. The bullet smacked into the framework of the doorway, the slight recoil made her flinch back, and in that second, Cellini darted forward into the room.

McNamara was actually on the floor, helpless; Jacob was

as helpless in that split second, his shoulders pushing against the wall, his feet slipping from under him. In full sight of both men, Cellini disappeared into the room and closed the door behind him.

Inside, Anne had recovered, and her gun was poised again. Cellini, despite this, turned his back on her, and calmly relocked the door.

That done, he turned to face Anne, who was gaping at him, the gun now drooping.

"Let me have that," he said, "and we can talk."

On the instant, she backed farther away.

"Stay there!" she ordered. "Don't move or I'll shoot you. Don't move."

"You know," said Cellini, patiently, "if you shoot me you won't have any chance at all of getting your husband back. You would spend a long time in prison and he and Vanessa could live together here or anywhere they liked. Isn't it time you faced facts, Mrs. Stone? There might be ways of getting your husband back, but this certainly isn't one."

She still covered him with the gun.

"What do you mean?"

"I mean that if you go on like this, you'll drive him farther away."

"He was coming when you stopped him. He was coming back to me!"

"Even if he came back, under that kind of pressure, he would live with you in hate."

"He wouldn't hate me! He wouldn't. It's the hold that woman has on him, that's the trouble, and you know it."

"I don't know anything of the kind," denied Cellini, and he moved forward. "Give me that gun."

"Keep away from me or I'll shoot you."

Cellini said, without any change of tone: "All right, Mrs.

Stone, if you'll feel happier, keep the gun. May I sit down?" He moved to a chair and lowered himself into it. "Ah, that is better. I am not so young as I used to be!" That sally was greeted with a frown that was nearly a scowl. "Now, supposing we start from the beginning. Do you *really* want your husband back?"

"You bloody fool, what do you think I'm doing this for?"

"Well," said Cellini, after a moment's consideration, "it could be for three reasons. It could be because you know you've lost him, but rather than let him find happiness with another woman you would kill him first and then yourself. That seems to me the most likely reason: that like many women you have a passionate hatred for anyone who could take your husband from you; when Congreve said that hell has no fury like a woman scorned, it was a simple statement of fact. There are the other possible reasons, however. One, that you want to drive your husband to distraction so that in order to free himself from you he will pay you a very large sum of money —"

"Don't you dare say that!" she interrupted fiercely.

"Whether you realise it or not, it is a possibility," Cellini insisted, quite calmly. "There is the third possible reason also, that you may in fact want to be free of him, want to leave him, but wish him to shoulder all the blame." When she didn't answer but simply stared, the pistol still pointing towards the floor, he crossed his legs and went on calmly: "Of course there is a fourth possible explanation, too."

Between her teeth, Anne demanded:

"So there's a fourth reason, is there? Well, don't just sit there. Tell me what it is!"

"That you are mad," said Dr. Cellini, with great deliberation. "After all, that was really why I was consulted: to find out whether you are sane or mad, and if mad, whether I can help you."

She stood some ten feet away from him, the gun slowly rising so that it was aimed at his chest. Her fingers were unsteady. Her right forefinger was on the trigger. If she fired she could not miss him; and if she hit him the wound might well be fatal.

Emmanuel Cellini stood unmoving in the face of death.

* * *

Outside, ears strained to catch every syllable, stood Jacob and McNamara. There was the sound of movement at the foot of the stairs, but that seemed part of another world, and the only world was the one beyond the locked door.

Each waited for the sound of a shot.

Each held their breath.

As second after second passed, the hope that Anne would not shoot grew stronger, but there could be no certainty, and both men knew that if they moved, or made the slightest sound, they might precipitate the shooting.

Still there was only silence from the room.

Quietly, but making some noise, a man came up the stairs behind them. This was Superintendent Hardy. He was followed by big Detective Sergeant Wallerby, who made no sound at all.

Chapter Seventeen

THE SIGHTSEERS

Chief Detective Superintendent John Hardy strode along the drive of King's House, aware immediately of an atmosphere of crisis. The road leading from the village, which was now almost a town in its own right, was lined with cars, and several policemen were controlling the traffic. A number of people were gathered about the drive and outlying trees. Men and women, all at leisure, children of all ages, mostly happily at play; and hippies presumably of both sexes, long-haired, mild-mannered, as curious as the rest. There was even an ice-cream van, with a line of children waiting patiently to be served. Newspapermen hovered, nearer the gate. Hardy, with a local plainclothes detective to guide him, watched all this tight-lipped.

There were several people on the open drive, not simply among the trees which separated the house and ground from the road. Hardy touched his horn and sent a couple of long-haired youths darting back. A third youth walked defiantly on. He did not move aside even when the drive widened into the carriageway.

Hardy, at last able to pull up alongside, asked in a voice which did not betray his anger:

"Do you live here?"

This youth's hair was not really long, but it looked

unkempt. Resentment lay in the shadowed eyes that, trouble-free, would have looked bright and attractive.

"Who wants to know?" he demanded, half-sneering.

Hardy turned to his guide.

"Officer, charge this man with trespass, take him to the station and hold him."

Hardy drove up as near the house as he could, watched by all three youths. The officer by him jumped out of the car, opened Hardy's door, and then turned towards the youths.

Two of them retreated.

The surly and defiant one walked on towards the house.

Hardy went up to the porch, where Wallerby stood talking to Dulcie. There was the sheen of alarm in the woman's eyes.

"But there *isn't* another way up to the room," she insisted. "Just the door and the windows."

"Surely through the ceiling —" began Wallerby.

"What's the use of telling you if you won't believe me?" the woman demanded, obviously very close to tears.

Her gaze flickered towards Hardy and Wallerby became aware of this new presence. He started, and drew himself up.

"Good afternoon, sir," he said, and looked slightly embarrassed. "I'm Wallerby."

"Hallo, Wallerby." Hardy nodded, and his manner immediately put the other man at his ease. "What's this about a room you can't get into?"

"I keep *telling* him," the woman almost sobbed. "It's the turret room, there's only one door and the windows, and they're shuttered, bolted and barred. There *isn't* any other way into it. Oh, dear God, what are we going to do?"

"Who's in the room?" Hardy asked Wallerby.

"Mrs. Stone is!" cried the woman.

"And Dr. Cellini," said Wallerby, flatly.

Hardy felt a sudden, sickening shock. It was a long, long

time since he had first met Cellini, almost as long since they had first become friends, and throughout the whole of their association Hardy had marvelled not only at Cellini's wisdom and his shrewdness, but also at his physical courage. It was his professional task to try to help the mentally deranged, and there were many who owed their present sanity to the help and guidance of Cellini at a time when they had hovered on the borderline of insanity. There were occasions when he appeared to take almost wild chances with his patients: when he forced them to come to grips with themselves in a way which would have frightened many a lesser man. But there were other patients, some dead, some shut away, whom he had not been able to help; and all of these had been prone to moods of great violence. And it was Cellini's way, when he became aware of this, to try to confront them himself: to draw the rage, the poison, out of their systems. Challenged, he would say simply that he was more likely to have a calming effect than friends or relatives, and no doubt that was true.

But it often meant taking risks far beyond the normal call of duty.

As Wallerby told Hardy that Cellini was with the woman, he had a swift mind picture of the older man, of his frailty. But there was more to Cellini, even in physical strength, than most people realised.

"Is she violent?" Hardy asked.

"She threatens to be, sir."

"Armed?"

"Yes, sir — apparently the turret room is a kind of armoury."

Hardy glanced at the woman and checked an impulse to say: "There must be a way in." At that moment another woman appeared from the passage alongside the wide staircase, a younger fair-haired woman with rare attractiveness, who moved beautifully. Hardy recognised her on the instant as Sir David Belhampton's daughter; so Wallerby was right. Hardy, who was the last man to defer to social rank as such, nevertheless felt the tensing of awareness. Sir David was a power behind the scenes in political affairs, an independent often revered and sometimes feared by both the major parties. He had been chairman of a Commission of Enquiry into the working of the police forces in Great Britain a few years before, and was known as a close friend of the present Home Secretary who, being the Senior Minister in charge of Home Affairs, was the Minister in charge of the police. In a way, Hardy's reaction to Belhampton was something akin to Wallerby's to Hardy. Consideration for the man would not make him budge an inch from any course he ought to take, but he would hate to earn Belhampton's disapproval.

Vanessa Belhampton drew up.

"Dulcie," she said, "I think you should come and relax for half an hour."

"But how can I?" wailed Dulcie. "With all this going on?"

"You won't be any use to Mr. or Mrs. Stone if you go on like this," Vanessa said. "Go and make some tea, I'd love a cup. I'll be along with you in a few moments." The tone of authority was so positive that Dulcie moved off obediently, and Vanessa, keeping her voice low, asked: "Is there any change in the situation upstairs?"

"I'm afraid not," said Wallerby. "Er — this is Superintendent Hardy, Miss. Superintendent, Miss Vanessa Belhampton."

Both murmured an acknowledgment. Vanessa went on:

"Superintendent, I beg you to find a way of getting both Dr. Cellini and Mrs. Stone out of that room safely."

"I beg you..." Her very heart was in her voice and in her eyes.

"If it can be done, we'll do it," Hardy promised her. "I'd

better go upstairs." He smiled, and turned away, and Wallerby hurried after him. Hardy was already aware of great tensions here; in Belhampton's daughter, in Wallerby, in the crowd outside. With Belhampton's daughter involved, this would hit every newspaper headline in the country.

"Straight up, along the passage and up the second flight of stairs," Wallerby explained, and when they were half-way up the stairway, he went on: "Mr. Stone and Dr. McNamara are outside the room, sir. I think I did mention Dr. McNamara over the telephone."

"Yes."

"I — er — I'm not too familiar with the situation, sir," went on Wallerby, "but I think both Miss Belhampton and Mr. Stone feel — feel responsible, sir."

"I see what you mean," replied Hardy, as they plodded upwards.

Outside the tall, solid-looking door at the far end of the landing above, stood two men. They both glanced round. In the taller man's face was anxiety as great as Vanessa Belhampton's; in the shorter, more powerful man there was burning impatience. From the room itself there was no sound. There were whispered introductions touched with a solemnity which was nearly absurd, before Hardy asked in a quiet voice: "Have they spoken recently?"

"Not for several minutes," Stone replied.

"We've got to break that door down," McNamara said hoarsely. "There's no other way."

Almost at once Anne called out: "If you do, I'll shoot this old man first, and myself afterwards. I want my husband, do you understand? That's all I want — my husband."

Hardy called back: "How can your husband come in, if the door is locked?"

"Who's that?" demanded Anne, her voice rising. "That's a voice I don't know. Who is it?"

"I am Superintendent Hardy of New Scotland Yard," Hardy answered. "Are you all right, Manny?"

There was hardly a pause, before Cellini replied: "I am perfectly all right, John, thank you. And I will be much obliged if —"

"I've got a gun," the woman called out. "I'll shoot him if anyone tries to get in."

". . . if you will leave us alone for a while," Cellini finished. "I think Mrs. Stone will be quite reasonable."

"Reasonable!" Anne screeched. "There's a woman in this house ready to walk off with my husband, and you expect me to be reasonable! Why, I'll blow your brains out!"

"God!" gasped Wallerby.

"Oh, my God," muttered McNamara, and he launched himself against the door.

"Don't fire that gun!" cried Jacob.

Hardy stood with his fists clenched by his sides, and at that moment, like a knell of doom, there came the sharp crack of a shot, followed by another, then by a sound like that of a body falling; and finally, silence. Hardy's heart was thumping wildly, the other men looked appalled, and there was a low-pitched gasp from the head of the stairs, from Vanessa.

Hardy opened his mouth to call: "Manny," but before he did so, Cellini spoke in an unflustered voice:

"You really mustn't, Mrs. Stone — if you kill me, as I have already warned you, you will spend much of your life in prison and your husband will be quite free to live with Miss Belhampton or any woman he pleases. May I make a suggestion to you?"

Hardy was sweating.

Wallerby muttered under his breath: *"My God, he's cool."*

Vanessa reached Jacob Stone's side, and as they gripped

hands, said: "We can't let him suffer for us, Jacob. We simply can't do it."

"Do you think Cellini's taking this risk for fun?" asked Hardy, his voice and manner suddenly fierce. "He wouldn't do this if he didn't think he had a chance to help Mrs. Stone."

Over these words, Anne said to Cellini in a voice all of them could hear: "What's this about a suggestion?"

"I wonder if you will really listen to one," Cellini said, still calmly.

"Try me," Anne said. "Go on, try me."

* * *

Ah, thought Cellini, she will listen.

He was as calm as he appeared to be, although for a few moments, when she had squeezed the trigger and could so easily have killed him, he had known cold fear. But both bullets had missed, passing within inches of his head, and he had soon recovered his poise. He had, now, little doubt about the truth; the problem was to find a way of bringing it out without anyone getting hurt. It would be touch and go, he was quite sure of that; one false move and he might not live to try again.

"Go on!" she screamed. "Make your suggestion!"

"Very well," said Cellini. "But first put the gun down."

"That old trick," she sneered.

"Really," said Cellini, and for the first time he sounded impatient, "how do you expect me to help you if at any moment you might kill me. I have never known such an unreasonable woman. No wonder your husband is tired of you."

"*What did you say?*"

"I said it was no wonder that your husband tired of you," said Cellini. "There is no sense in you. Are you going to put that gun down and listen to what I have to say, or are you going to go about uttering wild threats and waving the gun in my face? Good gracious! I have never been in such a situation. I wish I had never come to see you."

He stopped, the echoes of his voice fading.

Anne stood only two or three feet away from him, the pistol still in her hand. She looked puzzled. White-faced and tense, but puzzled. She breathed heavily, and her body twitched from time to time. If she did shoot again, there was little chance that she would miss.

"Tell me what your suggestion is," she said at last.

"When you've put the gun down."

"Do you think I'm a fool?"

"Yes," answered Cellini very crisply. "I do indeed. I think by your folly you have come near to throwing away a wonderful chance of happiness — and throwing away so much more. This home, for instance. The love and affection of your husband. The respect, no doubt, of many of your friends. Yes indeed, I do think you are a very foolish woman, Mrs. Stone."

"Why, I'll kill —"

"Oh, don't be silly," interrupted Cellini, tersely. "If I die, I die. I am an old man without much of life yet. I shall die in a few years, anyway. Whereas a young, beautiful and desirable woman like you wasting away in prison when you could have such a full life would be madness. Foolish?" he laughed. "It's utter madness!"

* * *

"He's incredible," muttered Wallerby.

"What is he trying to do?" breathed Jacob.

"Be quiet," breathed Vanessa.

It's touch and go, thought Hardy, anguished. Even for Manny it's touch and go.

McNamara stood with his hands clenched, breathing hard. Downstairs, Dulcie and the gardener's wife sat talking, policemen stood about. Outside the crowd grew thicker, while two policemen walking on the grass to deaden all sound, carried ladders to the turret and ran them up slowly and quietly to the shuttered windows.

* * *

Anne asked in a strange voice: "What do you mean by a full life?"

"I mean a life of enjoyment, of pleasure. How old are you, Mrs. Stone?"

"I — I am forty-five."

"Have you yet reached the menopause?" asked Cellini.

"No, I haven't, I — *why do you want to know?*"

"You behave rather as if you had. However —"

"Well, I haven't!"

"Then you have an even longer period of potential happiness ahead of you. Did you know that the forties and fifties can often be and should be the best years of a woman's life? When she can enjoy all the pleasure of sex without the responsibilities or the anxieties caused by the Pill, and —"

"Why are you talking to me like this?" she cried. "What are you trying to do?"

"I am trying to show you that there is no reason to kill yourself, and every reason to live," answered Cellini.

"The only reason I've got for living is my husband. If you're so clever, find a way to make him come back to me. Go out, and work your miracle there!" She moved forward and actually pushed him towards the door.

"If you need your husband so much," said Cellini in his most reasoning manner, "why did you try to kill him? Why did you knock him into the swimming pool?"

She went still and silent; and seemed to hold her breath. At last she spoke, more calmly than she had before since he had entered the room.

"*I* didn't try to kill him," she stated. "Whoever said I did is lying. I would gladly kill that bitch of a woman but I wouldn't hurt Jacob."

Chapter Eighteen

LIE?

Vanessa whispered: "Jacob."
"But I saw her," Jacob gasped.
"Are you sure?" Vanessa asked urgently.
"I — *saw* her —" Jacob began.
"*Be quiet!*" urged Hardy.
"We've got to get that door down!" cried McNamara.
"*Quiet!*" rasped Hardy, and he gripped McNamara's arm. In spite of his hoarse breathing McNamara fell quiet, as did the others, although there was fresh tension which affected them all like an electric shock. Vanessa slowly let go her hold on Jacob, who stared at her as if in horror.
Then, clearly, came Cellini's voice again.
"Or is it you who are lying?" he asked.
"Of course I'm not," Anne answered. "Who said I tried to kill Jacob? Who was it?"
Cellini answered: "Jacob himself."
"Oh, *no*," gasped Anne, in anguish.
"He said that he was standing by the pool last night, and you struck him over the head and knocked him in."
"He couldn't lie about me, whatever else he would do," said Anne. "It's not true. He didn't say that."
"He did, Anne," Cellini insisted.
"Oh, dear God, no," Anne gasped. "It's not true, it can't be

true. I saw him go out. I went out after him, I wanted to plead with him again, but I didn't strike him. I swear it!" Suddenly her voice rose: "Jacob, it's not true, tell them it's not true!"

* * *

"Jacob," breathed Vanessa.
"What the hell are you up to?" McNamara demanded, swinging round on Jacob.
"*Jacob!*" Anne screamed from the other side of the door, "tell them it's not true!"
"Jacob, Jacob," Vanessa almost sobbed. "Did you see her? Please don't lie. Did you see her?"
"You couldn't have seen me," called Anne, desperately. "Jacob, you couldn't. Oh, God," she gasped. "I'd rather kill myself. I'd have killed myself a hundred times, I'd rather he had a thousand women than kill him. Jacob! Please don't lie, whatever you do. I love you. I love you more than life itself. I couldn't live without you, I *swear* I didn't try to kill you."
Now, outside the door, Jacob sensed the doubting, near-accusing gaze of all the others on him. And all of a sudden, Vanessa seemed to be a million miles away.

* * *

Outside, in the grounds, the ladders were close to the windows of the turret room. The crowd among the trees was much thicker. A police car stood outside the house. There were more policemen and at least a dozen newspapermen and photographers. People were talking, there was a monotonous undertone of voices. Not far from the front door a child began to cry, and nearer at hand a man laughed. Someone said sternly: "Stop that."

* * *

Inside the turret room, Cellini looked at Anne Stone's face, seeing an expression which had not been there before. *Horror.* She was now looking towards the door, and he moved so that he could see her better. She was almost crying. The gun, still in her hand, pointed towards the floor. He moved towards her and, with the gentlest of movements, took it from her. She did not even seem to notice.

"Jacob!" she sobbed, "tell them it's not true, you didn't say I tried to kill you."

Tell *me* it's not true, Cellini echoed in his mind. How she wanted reassurance, how desperate she was for that.

He reached the door, and turned back the key. There was no sound from outside, except of heavy breathing. He turned the handle, and as he did so there was a sudden commotion on the landing, and there was McNamara, throwing himself at Jacob, who backed away in alarm. Hardy made a grab at the doctor but McNamara flung him off, and all the time muttered in a hoarse voice:

"You liar, you said she attacked you, you bloody liar!"

"*Sean!*" screamed Anne, and rushed towards them, but Cellini blocked the doorway and she could not get past.

Wallerby woke suddenly to action. In a flash he had McNamara by the shoulders. As McNamara's hold on Jacob slackened, Jacob pulled himself free. Then and only then Cellini stood aside. Anne rushed to Jacob, flinging her arms round him. She raised her face towards him in piteous entreaty.

"Jacob, tell me it wasn't me. Oh, dear God, if it was me I didn't know what I was doing. Oh, Jacob, I love you so, I love you so. Don't leave me, I beg you, don't leave me." She fell slowly, sliding down his body, until she was at his feet, her arms about his knees, her face still upturned, tears spilling from her eyes, the words faltering from her lips. "Don't leave me, please, whatever you do. I can't live without you. I would rather kill myself." She turned her head and looked up, now, at Vanessa, and she pleaded: "Don't take him away from me. I don't care how often he sees you, I don't even care if you come to live here, but don't take him away, let me have part of him. *Please,* Vanessa, *please.*"

Into a strange, deep pool of silence, Vanessa said: "I won't take him from you, I promise."

"Anne," said Jacob, "I won't leave you." He stooped down, to raise her up, putting his hands beneath her arms.

"It wasn't me," she sobbed. "It couldn't have been me." As he raised her she looked at Cellini. "If I did such a thing I wasn't sane, I wouldn't harm him. I swear I wouldn't. Please," she pleaded again, and now she stretched out one arm towards him. "Please tell me I'm not mad. I may have had a blackout, but I'm not mad, I —"

"You are not mad, Anne Stone," said Cellini, very clearly. "I assure you of that."

"Oh, thank God," she gasped. "Thank God."

"And you didn't attack your husband," Cellini said, as clearly.

The words seemed to run through the others like an electric shock, making all of them, including Vanessa, start violently. In a voice only just audible, Vanessa whispered:

"Oh, Jacob."

Jacob said in a husky voice: "But I *saw* her."

*   *   *

And he was sure.

He could picture the scene now. The starlit darkness. The quiet. The reflection of the stars in the pool. The rippling pool. The faint noises, as of the wind rustling through the trees, the movement which seemed so close. He could almost feel his sudden flare of fear, feel the swiftness of his movement, see the upraised arm falling.

He had seen her.

He was sweating, and was very cold at the neck and at the forehead; hot and cold over the rest of his body. Could he have been mistaken? Vanessa seemed to think — *Vanessa* seemed to think — that he had deliberately lied. And now Cellini said, as if he were absolutely sure, that Anne had not attacked him. After a moment his mind began to work. How *could* Cellini be so sure? The thought was no sooner in his mind than the question came.

"How can you say that, Cellini?"

"How can you say I *did?*" asked Anne, in a choky voice.

"Because I *saw* you. Good God, do you think I'd lie? I saw you in the grounds a few minutes before you hit me."

"I didn't hit you!"

"Be quiet!" Jacob suddenly roared, and he brought silence upon them all. "You were in the grounds — over by the tennis court shrubbery. Do you deny that?"

"No, I was there, but —"

"You wore a white scarf, the big one you always wear at night when you go out."

"Yes, I did, but —"

"You were wearing it when you crept up behind me." Jacob spoke as he felt, with absolute certainty, and confidence came slowly: he could not be wrong.

"Mr. Stone," Hardy interrupted.

"Can't you keep quiet while I finish?" Jacob rasped.

"No," said Hardy. "In case you have forgotten, I am a police officer, and you are discussing a crime — a very grave crime."

"I didn't hit him!" Anne sobbed.

"I tell you I saw you," Jacob insisted.

"Mr. Stone," began Hardy, and when Jacob raised his arms impatiently, he broke off. "Would you prefer to be questioned at the police station, sir?"

At last Jacob subsided, and Hardy went on:

"Mr. Stone, when you heard the sound behind you, was it dark?"

"Yes."

"Was there any light from the house?"

"A little, but the house is some distance from the pool."

"Is there a light at the pool?"

"Yes. But it wasn't switched on."

"You turned round very quickly, didn't you?"

"Yes. I was scared — and I had reason to be."

"Indeed you did. Did you see your wife's face?"

Jacob caught his breath. His gaze shifted to Anne, who was looking at him with desperate intensity.

"I — I saw the scarf," he replied gruffly.

"Did you see her face?"

"I — I'd seen her only a few minutes before, wearing the scarf. I could have sworn —"

"I *didn't strike you!*" cried Anne.

"Someone did. That scarf —"

"I'd gone indoors. I gave up hope. I'd gone indoors," Anne sobbed.

"Did you take the scarf off, Mrs. Stone?" asked Hardy.

"Yes, I — I always do."

"Before you get upstairs?"

"Yes, I keep it in the hall drawer, I only put it on when I go in the garden. Twigs from the trees catch in my hair."

"Do you remember putting it away last night?"

"Yes, I tell you!"

"So, someone else could have taken it out of the drawer, put it on, and then come out to the swimming pool and

attacked you." When Jacob didn't answer immediately, Hardy went on: "Couldn't that have happened?"
"I suppose so — yes! It could have happened!"
"And who knew where to find the scarf?"
Now, Anne said stonily: "Jacob knew."
"Jacob didn't strike himself."
She said: "Yes. I — I mean no. No, he —"
"Who else knew?"
Anne Stone was clutching her throat.
"I — I don't know."
"Who else knew?" demanded Hardy, his voice suddenly booming out. "Tell us, Mrs. Stone."
With a deep intake of breath, Anne whispered: "Dulcie."
"Dulcie!" echoed Vanessa.
"Dulcie?" Jacob said, in an unbelieving voice.
"Dulcie — often got it for me."
"Dulcie!" exclaimed Vanessa. "But why should she attack you? It doesn't make sense, she — you always said she was so loyal, she'd known you all her life. Not Dulcie."
"Who else knew?" insisted Hardy.
"No — no one. Except —"
"Did Dr. McNamara know?" asked Cellini, quietly. He did not put his thoughts into words, but there was much in Dr. McNamara's manner which needed explaining. His wild behaviour, his extraordinary emotion. Cellini did not understand the doctor except that he knew he was under great pressure.
"He — he may have been here."
"But did he?"
"What's the point in beating about the bush?" demanded McNamara in a harsh voice. "Yes, I knew. But if you think I put the scarf on and attacked Jacob you're wrong. God knows I'd like him out of the way, but murder — anyone who thinks I would commit it is wrong, absolutely wrong."

He was glaring.

"You want *me* out of the way?" asked Jacob, unbelieving.

"Oh, you never knew," Sean McNamara said. "And nor did Anne, I kept it from you both. I've loved her for so long it hurts to think of it. Even when my wife was alive, I loved Anne. There was no hope for us. Even if my religion had made it possible, my profession didn't. I was her doctor, your doctor, the family doctor. While my wife was alive I dared not even hope. When she died, I began to hope but I could not act or say a word. How could I? Answer me that! How could I?"

Cellini said softly: "Being you, you could not." And there was a world of understanding and of admiration in his voice.

McNamara said tersely: "Jacob, you must know whether it was a man or a woman. *Was it me?*"

Jacob said in an unsteady voice: "No. It —" he broke off. "No, it was —" His gaze turned towards Anne and he actually put his hands out towards her. "Anne, I'm sorry, but it *was* you. I did see you. It was your nose and your chin. I *saw* you. I wasn't lying and I wasn't imagining it. You were behind me."

He had no doubt at all and his certainty sounded in his voice and showed in his manner. And now he took Vanessa's arm, and she did not draw away from him.

"Oh, dear God," Anne gasped. And she stood up. She looked about her piteously, not for help, but in confusion. "I didn't know what I was doing. I swear I didn't know. I don't want to kill you. I'd do anything for you." She moved towards Cellini, and went on with hardly a pause: "I couldn't help it. I didn't know what I was doing. I —"

Cellini moved forward and took her hands, and asked very gently: "I know you didn't attack Jacob, Anne. Who are you protecting? You know who it was, don't you?"

"No!" she cried. "I didn't know what I was doing! I was temporarily insane, I couldn't help it."

"Anne," said Cellini, "I don't believe you struck your husband."

"But I did."

"Jacob," Cellini said, swinging round, "from which side were you attacked?"

"From the right side, my right side," Jacob answered, startled.

"You saw the upraised arm?"

"I've told you, I saw the head and the face and the stick!"

"And the arm?"

"No, not very well, it was dark. I inferred an arm was holding the stick —" Jacob broke off, suddenly, obviously appalled. "Oh, dear God," he said. "She had on a sleeveless dress at dinner. Her — her arms must have been bare. If — if she'd struck me I would have seen her arm."

There was a deathly silence.

And then, without the slightest warning, Anne Stone collapsed.

As she fell, McNamara rushed towards her and went on his knees; and none could doubt that it was not as a doctor but as a lover.

Chapter Nineteen

A MATTER OF TRESPASS

It was McNamara who lifted Anne and carried her into her room, Vanessa following. Dulcie, hurrying up the stairs, called by Wallerby, also went into Anne's room. As the group broke up, Cellini gripped Jacob's hands in reassurance, and said:
"We are not needed here, just now. May we go to your study?"
There was the study, with the window shattered; but the glass had been picked up and carried off somewhere, the tea trolley was gone, whisky, soda, water and glasses stood by Jacob's chair. A cool wind came in from the gaping window, but not enough to make the room cold. Jacob went to the drinks.
"Will you have a drink?" He unstoppered the whisky decanter.
Hardy was staring at a photograph of Anne, on the mantelpiece; a picture taken with the two girls and Anthony, fifteen years ago. There was another, much later, picture of the three children.
"Superintendent!" Jacob's voice was louder. "Will you have a drink?"
Hardy turned round.
"I don't think so," he said. "Thank you all the same.

There are some things I must talk to the local police about. You'll be here when I get back, Manny, won't you?"

"Yes," promised Cellini.

Hardy moved out of the room, and Detective Sergeant Wallerby appeared in the doorway, half a head taller, at least two inches broader than Hardy. As Jacob poured out a whisky for himself, impatiently, Hardy was asking in his quiet, unflurried way:

"Can you get the crowd away, Sergeant? There won't be any sensations for them now."

"We can get them out of the grounds," Wallerby replied. "They're trespassing all over the place. And if they're blocking the road we can move them from there, too."

"Do that at once," Hardy said.

His voice faded. Jacob drank half of his whisky and soda at a gulp, and then said gruffly: "Won't you have a drink, Dr. Cellini?"

Cellini, like Hardy, was looking at the photographs. Turning, he said: "A very weak whisky and water will be most welcome." As Jacob began to pour out, he went on: "Your children look very happy in this photograph, Jacob."

"Much of the time they were," Jacob said. He took the drink across, and picked up the photograph of the three children. "This was taken just before Angela got married. It was the last one of all three taken together. In a way, that was the beginning of the end for Anne and me. While the family was together we held on, but once Angela had gone, we just fell to pieces. Joan was married and away within a year, and Anthony — well, I told you about him." His tone was full of pain, his eyes seemed to burn. "Dr. Cellini, I was absolutely sure that Anne attacked me."

"And I am equally sure you were."

"If — if you could convince Vanessa —" Jacob began.

"It's all right, darling," Vanessa said from the foot of the

"Darling, you haven't heard a word Dr. Cellini said!"

"No," agreed Jacob, without hesitation. "Not a word. I'm sorry, I've been coming out of my trauma. Someone *did* knock me into the pool. If Anne didn't and it wasn't Sean McNamara, who was it?"

Cellini finished what was left of his drink, and put his glass down on the mantelpiece. Vanessa was quick to sense his change of mood. Jacob's arm tightened about her waist, as he, too, sensed the change in Cellini, saw the expression on that usually gentle face become forbidding, ominous.

"You were so sure it was Anne," he said flatly.

"Yes, but we know now that it wasn't."

"Who else is so like Anne that, in the darkness, with head shrouded, they might be mistaken for her?" asked Cellini. When Jacob did not answer, he went on: "Who left you in fierce anger, Jacob? Who left your home saying that he hated you? Who could make Anne lie to save him, changing gradually from flat denials to fearful confession? Who is there who could so affect your wife, Jacob?"

"Oh," Vanessa said, in an anguished voice. "Oh, my darling."

Jacob was staring across the room at the photograph on the mantelpiece, the last photograph taken of the children together at home. He went very pale, and seemed too shaken to look at Vanessa or at Cellini. They were standing there when a sound of a car came from outside. The engine stopped, the door slammed, footsteps sounded; heavy footsteps and light. Slowly, Jacob turned his gaze towards the doorway.

A youth appeared, unruly of hair, a burning directness about his eyes. He wore a pair of frayed and patched jeans, and a jacket with flowers emblazoned on it, some sewn, some stuck with tape, some embroidered. By his side was John Hardy.

"Mr. Stone," Hardy said, "this young man claims that he is your son."

There was tense silence, before the young man said in a cold voice: "I only told him because he said I was trespassing. Even you wouldn't accuse me of that, would you?"

Jacob gripped Vanessa so tightly that the pressure hurt.

There was utter silence; silence in which he seemed to see this boy as a baby, a child, a schoolboy and — as a young man. Now, at last he spoke very quietly.

"No, Anthony. Even I wouldn't do that. Why —" He broke off, closing his eyes. "It doesn't matter," he muttered. "Will you — will you go upstairs and see your mother?"

There was no immediate answer. Jacob opened his eyes, and saw his son move a little farther into the room, but Hardy had gone; and there was no other policeman, no sound or shadows of them. But there was Cellini, and somehow Cellini loomed larger than he had done, as if he had grown in physical stature until he almost took the place of Hardy, even of Wallerby.

"Before Anthony goes anywhere," he said, "I think we must clear the air of a number of doubts. Anthony — why did you come?"

"It doesn't matter," the youth answered.

"It matters a great deal."

"All right," Anthony said, in his brusque way, "it matters," He stopped there.

"Jacob," Cellini said. "I fear you have a most unpleasant task."

Jacob was staring at his son. Vanessa had freed herself and was standing on one side, watching the son, not the father.

"What task?" Jacob asked.

"You have to charge your son with attempting to murder you."

Jacob said in a strangled voice: "Was it you, Anthony?"
Very slowly and precisely, Anthony said: "Yes."
"Please — please tell me why."
"Why don't you do what your friend advises and charge me," Anthony asked, bitterly.
"Why did you try to kill me, Anthony?"
"I — I *didn't* try to kill you," the youth said roughly.
"But you struck me."
"That's right. I'd come to see my mother. I heard what you were talking about. I — I *hated* you." There was a long, long pause, and the boy's eyes burned, his lips seemed to quiver. "I couldn't talk to her, she was too upset. I — I just hated you. I followed you. When I saw you by the pool, I wished you were dead. I picked up a piece of wood. I hit you as hard as I could, if the weapon hadn't been so light I *might* have killed you. But — when you went in, I stood and watched. I didn't go away until I saw you were getting out of the water. If I'd had to I would have come and got you out. I — oh, God!" he cried. "I didn't want to kill you! Once I was on your side. Now I blamed you for what she had become, but I didn't want to kill you."
He stopped.
His whole body was ashake.
He did not move when his father stepped towards him.
"There is one peculiar thing," Cellini said, stopping Jacob. "Why did you wear your mother's scarf?"
The boy didn't answer.
"Tell me, Anthony," Cellini urged. "Only the simple truth will serve, now."
Anthony said in a cracking voice: "I wanted something of hers. I — I just took it out of the drawer, and went out, and wrapped it round my head the way she used to wrap a scarf round me when I was — when I was a kid. I — I just wanted something of hers."

Jacob said: "Oh, Anthony, Anthony, there is nothing of hers and nothing of mine you could not have."

Tears were filling Vanessa's eyes.

"Anthony," said Cellini, into the tension, "answer me one more question."

"What?"

"Why did you come here today?"

Anthony drew a deep breath, and his voice rose to a tone of desperation.

"I'd heard people in the pub saying *she* had tried to kill you. I couldn't let you believe it. I couldn't let her take the blame." Suddenly he seemed to crumple up, and he buried his face in his hands and began to cry. In a trice, Jacob went towards him, but there was a movement at the door, and Anne came in, McNamara hovering just behind her. Jacob drew back. And Anne stood in front of her son, and eased his hands away from his face, and cradled him so that his head rested against her breast.

* * *

"There was and there is no evil in King's House," Cellini said to Hardy, when they were at the police station, with Wallerby an eager third. "There was much misery but there may now be happiness to exorcise it. When I left, they were all talking together as if part of the same family — Anne Stone and Vanessa, Jacob Stone and McNamara; and Anthony, too. They will say much in the euphoria of the moment and moods will change and harden, while memories will bring back moments of resentment, but all of the problems arising from these things will be resolved."

"How do you think it will be resolved?" asked Wallerby. "Will Jacob Stone go back to his wife?"

"Oh, no," Cellini said emphatically. "That was a marriage which never should have begun. It was subconscious —

perhaps even conscious — awareness of the inescapable incompatibility of his parents which drove the son away. I think he will be happy when he visits either his mother or his father but there could be no happiness if they were together. There is talk of Jacob going to live in his club in London until the divorce is through, but more likely I think Anne will go and visit her daughters overseas while Jacob stays on at the house. Eventually she will marry McNamara. There is already talk that they will emigrate, once they are married. Perhaps even before. We shall see. They will have their problems, of course, each of them. By far the most remarkable person among them all is Vanessa Belhampton. I suppose, knowing her father, one should not be surprised. Meanwhile, you have nothing more serious than trespass for a charge, Sergeant! Certainly there will be no charge against Anthony; I think we can treat that as a family quarrel."

He gave a funny little quirk of a smile, and then went out, with Hardy, to his quaint, old, vintage car.

* * *

"Vanessa," Jacob Stone said, as he stood outside her house, late that night. "I didn't think I could ever be so content. And you?"

"More content that I've ever been," Vanessa assured him.

* * *

"Anne," Sean McNamara said for what must be the twentieth time. "I've been in love with you for years. It wasn't until I realised how things were between you and Jacob that I began even to dream of telling you so. It's an astonishing thing — I was the family's doctor for so long, I knew about the problems with the children but I didn't dream that you and Jacob were so acutely unhappy."

"Sometimes," Anne said. "I didn't realise it myself."

*   *   *

"If you ask me, Master Anthony, you ought to sleep in a comfortable bed for once," said Dulcie, severely.

"Not I!" declared Anthony. "I've a sleeping bag, and I'm going to sleep with my friends by the pool. I'll bring them all into breakfast in the morning!" And then his smile faded and he looked earnestly at Dulcie, almost pleadingly: "They will be all right now, won't they? You're sure they will?"

Out of her knowledge and her wisdom, Dulcie answered with a phrase which might have come from the lips of Dr. Cellini; and her tone was much like his.

"Yes," she said, "they'll be happy, because they don't hate any more. There's nothing as empty as hate."